G000055530

LEARNING TO LOVE

NEW ZEALAND SAILING BOOK 1

TRINITY WOOD

romance café
PUBLISHING

For everyone who wants to publish their work, and is still thinking about it.

I believe in you.

No wind blows right for the sailor who doesn't know where the harbor is.
~ Norwegian Proverb ~

GLOSSARY

Tui - The tui is a boisterous medium-sized bird native to New Zealand. It is blue, green, and bronze colored with a distinctive white throat tuft.

Kauri - Kauri are among the world's mightiest trees, growing to over 50 m tall, with trunk girths up to 16 m, and living for over 2,000 years.

Pounamu - Traditionally, pounamu, or greenstone (jade), is regarded as a talisman. Māori designs and symbols carved in pounamu carry spiritual significance.

Nikau - The Nikau is the only palm tree native to mainland New Zealand.

Pohutukawa - Also called the New Zealand Christmas tree, it's a coastal evergreen tree in the myrtle family that produces a brilliant display of red flowers.

Jibe - Also gybe, in sailing it means to change course by swinging the sail across a following wind.

Tim-Tam - Tim Tam is a brand of chocolate biscuit made by the Australian biscuit company Arnott's. It consists of two malted biscuits separated by a light chocolate cream filling and coated in a thin layer of textured chocolate.

Kawakawa - Kawakawa is a versatile herb and one of the most important in Māori medicine. It has been used traditionally to treat cuts, wounds, stomach and rheumatic pain, skin disorders, and toothache.

Kiwi - a flightless bird native to New Zealand, also a nickname for New Zealanders.

Ka pai, tamariki (Te Reo Maori) - Well done, children.

CHAPTER 1

SAM

The best ideas come to me when I'm on the water. Through the ocean expanse in front of me, the waves, or speeding through in a sailing boat, I can just *be*. The lingering stillness, the sun, the bird calls, the loud pounding of the surf have been my favorite music since I was a boy.

I lean against a doorway, fading evening sun on my face, drink in hand, and close my eyes, imagining I'm back on the water, my pulse slowing down …

"Stop hogging the doorway, Sam.". Gracie's impatient words snap me out of my reverie. I crash land back into the jam-packed house party on Auckland's North Shore. Too much noise. Too people-y. This is why I never go to parties.

Gracie rushes past me with what looks like a small mountain of vegetables ready to topple over. She drops them on the counter. "Come out of hiding and help Ellie here with the salads, and then we'll see you both outside. Shout if you need anything." With barely a glance over her shoulder, Gracie, ever the perfect hostess, waves towards the door. A woman, petite—can't be more than a few inches over five feet—curvy, hair dark velvet, eyes the color of an ocean sunset - just stands there as if she isn't some sort of sea goddess.

Who could notice any other damn thing with a whirlwind like Gracie flying through? No wonder I hadn't seen the girl trailing behind her, struggling with two large bowls. I hastily put my drink down, relieve her of the bowls, and clear some space on the counter.

The sea goddess named Ellie pushes hair behind her ear and smiles shyly. "Hey there. Gracie asked me to prepare some salads for the barbecue. She said you could help us out. Hope you don't mind." Ellie flicks her gaze in my direction then back down at the countertop.

Every word sounds a bit strained, like she is embarrassed. Or maybe afraid? I'm making her uncomfortable. I realize I'm staring and snap out of it. I'm not looking for a relationship. I'm not looking for anything casual, either. Corey says every time I start seeing someone, I fall. *Hard.* I might as well be a eunuch these days. But I won't be for much longer if I stay near the goddess. She tempts me too much, and maybe… if I turned on the charm, she'll say yes.

No. Gotta shut those thoughts down hard. I'll escape after dinner. Sooner if I can get these salads out of the way.

No escaping from the salads though. I put on my well-worn camera smile. "Sweet. What are we making? How can I help?"

My smile, albeit forced, seems to have put her at ease. She beams back, making my heart beat slightly faster. This is soooo not good news. Maybe if I went out more, I wouldn't have such a response to one pretty girl.

She points at one of the large bowls. "How about you wash the lettuce, then shred it into this bowl." She points at one of the large bowls. "I'll slice the rest of the veggies and make the vinaigrette. Then we'll put it all together, toss in some grilled halloumi, and we're ready to go."

She can cook, eh? My skills in the kitchen are limited to eggs on toast, so all this talk of vinaigrettes and halloumi is making me more nervous than the last World Sailing Championships when it looked like we were losing. Racing heart, shaky hands. Hopefully no puking, though. I avoid looking at her, pick up the lettuce and carry it to the sink. As the silence stretches and we work side by side, I contemplate briefly what it would be like to have someone to cook with, to live with. The thought passes as quickly as it came. I can't do it, and it would be foolish to pretend otherwise. I'm never at home. I don't have time for a relationship, and unlike Corey, I don't know *how* to keep things casual.

"I'm Ellie by the way," she says. "I don't think I caught your name, but you look familiar. Have we met before?" Her eyes narrow and her head tilts to the side, considering, likely, where she's seen me.

I'm fighting an urge to kiss her. "I don't think we've met before. I'd remember. Trust me." Just what the *hell* am I doing? For a moment I feel reckless, like I'm back on the water, and a big surge is coming towards me. Her smile is everything. Seems like I can't get enough of it. My flirting skills have always been subpar, but today I'm really feeling it. It sounds like a pickup line, but it's the truth. Just met her and I can't look away from her hair, her eyes, her lips. Damn, those lips. Her eyes widen, and her gaze flicks to my lips. And I'm less than a foot from her, leaning in as if I were about to kiss her. I pull back as if shocked.

"Then maybe I've seen you on TV. Reality TV shows? The News? Hmm ..." She puts the final touches to her masterpieces. They look more like works of art than salads. I feel loath to eat them.

Eating *her* up like the masterpiece she is, on the other hand ... My resolve is going downhill fast. Man, it's been a long time since I've dated or even been on a date. I should really go out more. I'm drooling like a teenager over someone I met ten minutes ago.

"Ahem?"

I've been lost in space yet again, and left her question hanging in the air between us. What time is it? If it's after 7 PM, maybe I can make an excuse and get away before I do something stupid.

"My name's Sam," I say. "I'm a sailor. I have a couple of days off, then I'm back with the guys on the water." Two days, but standing in this kitchen, in close proximity to Ellie, it feels like a lifetime away. Paddy told me time stood still when he met Gracie, but I laughed it off.

Well played Paddy, well played.

"Sam … I think I recognize you now! You're Sam Northcroft. From the sailing team." The tongs she's holding clatter to the countertop and she stares wide-eyed at me. "I'm not really into sailing, but you guys won the Olympics. That's an amazing achievement, huge thing for our country." She picks up one of the bowls, gestures for me to get the other one, and we make our way out to the barbecue area. I watch, mesmerized by the sway of her hips.

"Sam, bro, come here." The sunshine and Paddy's words shatter the spell, hurl me back to reality. I put the bowl down on the table and join Paddy at the barbecue. That's exactly what I need right now to get my mind off Ellie—Paddy and a bit of bullshitting. Some perspective would be good, too. And a lot of resolve.

I've been friends with Paddy since we were five. We went to the same school in O'Neills Bay, then our paths separated when I took up sailing, and he became a rugby pro. We met again recently, and it felt like we'd never been apart.

He's more than met his match in Gracie, who always managed to handle him through his ups and downs. I'm very happy to see him settled, it suits him, but it's obviously given me ideas I don't need.

I give him a pat on the back, just like in the old days. "Yo. What's up?"

"How's it going, bro? We never see you these days. You're always on the water. You need a woman to keep you on land, so we can see you more." He tries to poke me with the meat tongs.

I jerk away from the tongs and lightly punch his shoulder. These days it feels like everyone takes an interest in my love life, from my mum, to my brother, to my Nana who's got dementia and half the time doesn't remember who I am, to the newspapers.

I take a deep sigh. "Maybe I like mermaids."

"You're a meme now, bro. Saw it the other day, Sam's new girl. Picture of a seagull." He laughs so hard, I think he's going to choke. Maybe I *wish* he's going to choke. I scowl at him, then I spot Ellie in a corner talking with some girls. She's a bit shorter than the others, but she looks stunning, and I stare a bit longer than I should.

Paddy slides closer, looks the same direction as me. "Ah, so that's how the wind blows, bro. Alright, alright. Good one." He picks up the cooked meat, expertly lays it on a platter, and pushes it towards me. "Time for *kai.*"

Nope, it's time to *go.* The wind might push me towards Ellie the sea goddess - hell, she might even command the ocean winds to blow. But I can't follow. Not her. Not anyone. Not right now.

* * *

ELLIE

*I*f Gracie doesn't stop trying to set me up with random guys, I'm going to change my name and move to a different town. Take an active interest in my life, my ass. It was bad enough last week when she set me up with ... Marcus? Mark? Methuselah? See, I can't even remember! But this. This is almost like betrayal because I'm sitting next to THE Sam Northcroft, Olympic sailor (and salad maker, apparently), and he's not saying a word.

Earlier in the kitchen, when he looked at me with those smouldering eyes and said he'd have remembered me if we met before, I felt like we were THIS close to kissing. Now it's more like we're oceans apart.

I jump from the table, pull Gracie into a corner, lean in close. "Do you seriously think to hook me up with an Olympian?"

Gracie held her hands up, palms to the sky. "Why not? He's in his early thirties, so not too much older than you. And he's VERY single."

"VERY single. So there are degrees of singleness?"

Gracie nods. "Of course there are."

"Are there levels, then, like we're in a video game? Level One when you're just out of a relationship. Level Two means you're ready to date. And Level Three is … what? Casual dating? What level am I?"

"The level where you return to the table and talk to the very nice, very attractive, VERY single man."

I grunt, but return. *Very* single, huh? That likely means he is the no-commitment type. Makes sense. He's a sailor, not often on land. He probably doesn't have a pet. Or a plant. Or socks. Maybe he does have socks. He does appear on TV occasionally. How would he get on with Daisy? And more importantly, do I care?

What he does have is the ability to make me weak at the knees whenever I think of him. He's not my usual type, if I have a type. I scan his profile. Too rugged, too tall, too windswept. Just *too much*. And too *little* commitment. Why Gracie thinks we would make a good fit, apart from the fact we're both single, I'll never know, but the attraction is definitely there. I've not felt attraction like this in … ever. But attraction means nothing. Right? But what if it means something? I'll never know unless I try. What woman in her right mind would pass up a chance, no matter how small, with an Olympian? I gather my courage. Time to test the waters. "Hey stranger, we meet again." I'm not good at flirting like Tayla. She would have had him lusting after her by now.

"Hey yourself." He fixes his blue-gray gaze on me, then turns away quickly. Why is he so skittish? Am I making him as nervous as I'm feeling?

"How do you know Paddy and Gracie? I haven't seen you around here before."

He puts down his drink, and seems to relax a fraction. I get a glimpse of that crooked smile again. "I've known Paddy since we were kids. We went to the same school. Life got in the way, but recently our paths crossed again. He's a good one."

The chatter around us seems to increase, and instinctively we move closer to each other on the bench. Don't know what it is, his scent, the nearness of him, is maddening. I want more.

He's quite close now. I wonder if he'll make a move, but he seems so calm and collected, like nothing can ruffle him.

"How do you know them?"

"Friends of friends. Gracie is mates with my flatmate Tayla. She couldn't come here today. She's at a retreat." I can't stop babbling to keep the conversation going, yet his gaze never falls from mine. He watches me with quiet intensity, like every word coming from my mouth is a gem to treasure. We're surrounded by lots of people, but it feels like we're in a world of our own.

"What sort of retreat? Yoga, herbal teas, essential oils?" He smiles and makes a wide gesture encompassing all that stuff.

I bristle and turn to my plate feeling stiff. "Yoga retreat." It's clear from his dismissal he considers "all that stuff" airy-fairy, but it's dear to Tayla, so it's dear to me. I sniff and lift my chin.

"I'm not knocking it! My friend Corey's into that sort of stuff." He chuckles. "They're probably bound to meet at some point."

Through a haze I realize he's talking about his friend and sailing partner Corey Fine. From what I'd heard, Sam's like the Yin to Corey's Yang. One's quiet, broody, and awkward. The other one is cheerful, always puts a smile on the faces of everyone he meets.

Sam intrigues me, from his deep silences, to his eyes. They look like they carry a thousand secrets. And I want to know every single one of them. "Maybe we should set them up. They could put those essential oils to good use." I half laugh, half groan, mortified. My sense of humor is going to send him running for the ocean.

He just smiles wistfully and looks at his drink. "It's time for me to head off. I'll see if Paddy needs me for anything. Otherwise, I guess I'll see you around."

He stands and panic rushes through me. What if I never see him again? Asking Gracie for his number would be so embarrassing.

Paddy strides across the room and hangs an arm around Sam's shoulders. "Leaving already, bro? That was fast. Plus, you're leaving *alone*." He winks at me.

Not sure how to interpret that one. Has Gracie told him something?

Sam chuckles softly and gives Paddy a bear hug. "I'll leave my car at yours, and Uber home. Only had a couple of drinks, but I don't want to risk it." Strange that for someone who takes so many risks on the water, he seems so risk averse in his personal life. What is this man's secret?

"Ellie here needs a ride home. She lives about five minutes away from here on the Shore." Paddy is like a dog with a bone. I'm certain Gracie's sent him around to do her dirty work. I practically can hear her cackling all the way from the kitchen. "How about she drives your car to her place?"

One of Sam's eyebrows shoots up. "And where do I go?"

The plan is ridiculous. And so obvious. But I don't want to let him go. Not yet. "You come with me in the car to my place, have a coffee, sober up a bit, hang around, then take yourself home." I give myself a perfect ten for that mental gymnastics. Talk about twisted logic. After all, why can't he just crash at Paddy and Gracie's place and return home in the morning. Or just Uber home, wherever that is.

Paddy blows a chef's kiss. "Perfection. See you next time. Have fun and stay safe." He winks to us as he pushes us through pertiers, past a beaming Gracie, and out the door into the quiet of the driveway.

Sam's brows furrow. "What was that? I didn't understand any of it. Maybe I did have more to drink than usual." He shakes his head. "Ok, we'll go to your place, have a coffee to sober up, then I'll drive home when I'm ready." He looks at me apologetically and hands me the car keys.

He hasn't made any move towards me. I'm starting to think I've just imagined the whole thing, the desire, the closeness. I'll have to put this to the test.

I perk up and press the car unlock button to see which one it is. We get in, and I try to familiarize myself with the car. "Firstly, no car key holder. Interesting. Secondly, no handbrake. Even more interesting."

He watches me intently, a smile tugging at the corner of his lips.

"Is this the eject button? Every spaceship should have one."

Now he's outright laughing.

"Press this button, then this button, then we should be ready to go. There's a footbrake." When he leans over to show me how to make this ridiculous spaceship work, he puts a hand on my leg. The lightest touch, but it makes me weak at the knees. Again.

Sam's car roars into life, and I start my brief journey homeward with an all-consuming knot in my gut.

CHAPTER 2

SAM

*M*y car glides through the night past sleepy Shore streets lined with Pohutukawa trees, and my thoughts circle and swirl in my head like a riptide in the ocean.

I roll the window down and the fresh sea air hits me, its salty smell combined with something else. Is it the night-time? Is it anticipation?

I can't make head nor tail of why Ellie's driving us in my car to her house. I can't read physical, non-verbal cues very well at the best of times. Add that to the effect she has on my brain, and it's easy to see why I'm petrified of saying or doing something wrong. As always.

She looks so petite in the driver's seat, pulled forward as much as possible. Her dark hair is cascading over one tanned shoulder, and her hands grip the steering wheel a bit too hard.

I imagine her hands on me, her tanned legs around me. I look away and try to think of something else before she notices the effect she has on me.

She turns into a no-exit road with 50s style weatherboard Kiwi houses and stops outside the last one. "Here we are."

As we climb up the steps to the front door, I remember visiting my Nana in a similar house when I was a child. All native timber wooden floors, small rooms, and a giant fireplace in the living area. It didn't have a grate on the roof, and birds got trapped in it often. I rescued all of them.

She smiles. "Tayla's not in. She's coming back tomorrow from her retreat, but there's someone else inside." As soon as she turns the key in the lock, a bark erupts from the other side.

Ellie pushes the door open and a small beast rushes out. Ellie kneels to greet it. "Shhh, Daisy, it's late. This is Sam. He's a good guy." Ellie pats and comforts a small gray Staffordshire Terrier. Daisy laps up all the attention then comes to sniff me. I'm not a dog person, or a cat person, to be frank. They require too much commitment for someone who's always gone. I give Daisy two pats on the back, and she leaves content, tail wagging.

"She likes you." Ellie beams at me. Seems like I passed some sort of test. I follow her into the kitchen like a shadow. In her proximity, I feel too big, too awkward, too surly. Like on many occasions, I wish I had Corey's charm.

"... your coffee?"

What did she ask? I should have been listening to her question instead of looking at her like she's dessert. What does she taste like? I shake my head to try and focus. Maybe she asked how I like my coffee. "Milk, no sugar, please. Can I help?"

"Nah, you're alright. It'll be ready in a jiffy." She puts coffee grounds in the small French press then tops up with hot water, pushes the plunger, and pours two coffees. When she hands me a cup, our fingers brush and I feel it to my toes.

I scald my mouth trying to drink too fast. "For fuck's sake!" I put my cup down.

She's trying hard not to laugh.

In a couple of strides, I'm next to her.

She looks at me wide eyed, full lips slightly open.

I'm on the edge, barely holding on to whatever sanity I have left. "You're a witch. I'm under a spell of some sort." It's probably half true, as we stand close, neither of us daring to make a move.

"Maybe I'm a mermaid. Keep you coming back for more."

Something shatters inside me, and the recklessness that makes me feel free on the water surfaces.

My arms slide around her, pulling her closer, and I kiss her like I'm ravenous. She meets me all the way, so I lift her up on the counter. Her legs wrap around me, and her hands fist in my hair. A sense of urgency washes through me. This is more than want. This is *need*. Ellie is at the center of my universe, and the only thing I want to do is make her happy.

She breaks off the kiss. "Let's go to my room." She leads me to the end room of the house. There's a small double bed, some artwork on the walls, a ridiculously fuzzy plant, and Daisy snoozing on her dog bed. It's warm, cozy, and feels like home.

Ellie's hands are on me. "You're too dressed." Ellie takes my t-shirt off then pulls my shorts and boxers down, exposing my hard-on. Her small gasp makes me feel a thousand feet tall. I help her ease out of her top and shorts, leaving her in nothing but lingerie.

I'm already too far gone to care what she's wearing. She could have worn a mime outfit and I would have still found her sexy. I want to worship her from head to toe and make every inch of her body tremble with desire for me and no one else.

I free her breasts, and I suck her nipples, alternating

between them. God, I'm so hungry for her. She takes my hand and puts it between her legs. I can feel how wet she is through her undies.

Her thong can't come off quickly enough, and my fingers rest on her clit. Her body grinds against me, begging for release, so I dip one finger, then two fingers inside her. I start rubbing her clit with circular motions, until her body tenses, and with a moan she comes all over my fingers.

I'm so deep in desire I'm dripping pre-cum. She touches my chest and helps me slip a condom on, holding the head of my dick in a firm grip. I'm dying to be inside her. I kiss her swollen lips like my life depends on it. In a single quick motion I slide inside her, giving her a moment to adjust to the feeling. I can feel her squeezing my dick, and I know I'm not going to last long this time. I try to think about some-thing else, but I can't help myself, and I come deep inside her.

We lay in silence side by side, her dark hair fanned across my chest, but I'm still hard even after removing my condom. Her fingers gently stroke my chest, and I haven't had my fill of her.

Will it ever be enough?

I nuzzle her head, and feel her fingers make their way under the covers, wrapping around my dick.

Ellie looks up at me with a lazy smile. She slips another condom on my hard shaft then climbs on top and starts riding me. I hold on for dear life. Is this what heaven feels like? Her small breasts bouncing beg to be kissed, so I lift myself up and feast on her, then I lie on my back again, letting her grind against me. She circles her clit and moans, and I realize she is going to come before me. I arch my hips and pull her down to me so I'm deep inside her. And then she shatters, her head falling back, a moan ripping from her throat, her muscles clenching around me.

I put her down, and move on top again, knowing I'm very

close to coming. She's slick with wetness, and once I'm inside her, a wave rushes through me again. I come undone.

I feel like I've ran a marathon, heavy but strangely light. We fit together so well I don't want to move an inch. Next to her, I fall into a deep sleep, dreaming of the ocean.

ELLIE

*L*ast night felt a bit like a dream. Not a man of many words, my Sam. He's a man of action. Takes a while to get going, but once he starts, he doesn't stop. Strange I've come to think of him as *my* Sam. We haven't even been on a proper date together. Yesterday morning he was a stranger, someone I'd seen on TV a couple of times, and this morning he's asleep next to me in my bed. All surreal, like I'm living someone else's life.

Sam stirs in his sleep, spooning me closer, and his erection presses against me. This man's insatiable. He leaves a trail of small kisses on my neck, his fingers slow but persistent on the curve of my ass, caressing their way down my thighs and in between my legs. I feel myself getting wet again, craving his touch more and more. As the familiar sweet tension builds inside me, he moves his hand away, leaving me bereft.

Halfway between waking and sleep, my limbs are heavy, drowsy. They grow even heavier with desire, and I lay helpless beneath his touch. He spoons me again, and strokes my clit. Holding onto my hips, he pushes inside me slowly, and I can't stop a moan from escaping my lips. He's going to make me lose my mind. His large hand sears my hip, then his fingers rub my clit, his lips nuzzle my neck as his thrusting grows more urgent. I feel his dick stretch me even more, and I realize he's going to come. I don't think I can hold on any longer, and I surrender to the sensations engulfing me.

We lay in silence for a couple of moments, and I can't help but feel a little bit of sadness at seeing the light breaking through the window. It's tomorrow already. Sunday morning. He'll be on his way soon, and who knows when I'll see him again.

I turn to face him and smile, feeling shy despite everything that's happened between us. "Would you like some breakfast?" He blinks at me, then his gaze slides away from mine.

Not going to say anything, then? Fine, then. I leave his arms and the bed and put on a short robe.

He considers me with serious eyes. They might hold a hint of sadness, too. Maybe I'm imagining things.

"Nah, I'm alright. Thanks. I'd better get going. I'll shower at home." He gets up, puts on yesterday's clothes, and follows me to the front of the house without making any move to touch me or at least give me an inkling of what happened between us.

In the light of day, I suddenly feel shy. I don't think I've ever brought home a guy I'd only just met, but there's a first for everything. "Are you sure you don't want some cereal at least? Or just coffee?"

Sam looks at me, very conflicted, but he seems to have made a decision. "Ok, I'll have some cereal, then I'm definitely heading off."

"I bet you're ravenous." The words came out before I could stop them, so I try not to look at him while I prepare a bowl of Weetbix cereal with milk. Somehow, he doesn't seem the sugar add-on type.

He dwarfs our small kitchen table with his presence and gulps down large spoonfuls.

Daisy chooses that time to burst in through the doggy door and comes to me for rubs.

I sit on the floor, and start one of my usual chats with Daisy. "Have you been outside, Daisy-Boo? How's the weather? Any good digging this morning?"

Sam eats in silence, looking at us like we're not all there. "I don't know anything about you," he says quietly.

I raise my head. "What do you want to know?" I leave Daisy on the floor and sit next to Sam at the table.

"Everything."

I laugh, but he seems quite serious. He almost avoids looking into my eyes.

"Okay. Ellie Tennyson, 25 years old. Grew up North, towards Matakana. I'm a preschool teacher at Cheeky Monkeys in Takapuna. I like roses and chocolate. My favorite color is yellow. Just an ordinary girl, really."

He chuckles at that and continues eating. In the morning light, his hair looks a bit darker than last night. I want to ask him the same question he just asked me. I want to learn about his likes and dislikes, but the key turns into the lock, and Daisy bursts into action.

A voice calls out from the front door. "Ellie, there's an SUV outside blocking our driveway. I had to park right on the road. Feel like keying the motherfucker's car. He probably has the smallest dick ever and feels the need to compensate." Tayla, my flatmate, has chosen this very moment to come back home, and boy, she's huffing and puffing.

She sees Sam sitting at the table and her jaw drops. "I didn't know you had guests. I think I'll come back later." She mouths, "I'm sorry," gathers her duffel bags, and steps back in retreat.

Sam stands swiftly. "Nah, you're alright. It's time I went home. Busy day ahead." He strides to the door.

I realize I haven't given him my mobile number. Would feel a bit awkward asking Gracie for his. I quickly scribble my number on a corner of an old grocery shopping list and thrust it in his hand as he's about to exit through the front door. "Didn't give you my number. Here it is. Between the sausages and tomatoes." I keep my tone light, though I'm dying a little inside because I know deep in my soul he's probably not going to call or message me. Just like the rest of them.

He takes the scrap of paper. "Thanks. See you." He retreats to his car. No kiss, no hug, no acknowledgment of what happened last night. And this morning. He drives away without a second glance.

"What. The. Fuck. Was. That?" Tayla's sunglasses have fallen on her nose, her light pink hair looks wild, and her hands are on her hips.

I don't know what to say. The truth is probably better out. "We met at Gracie and Paddy's yesterday evening. We hit it off, he came here. Stayed the night. Now he's gone." I take away his bowl and pack it into the dishwasher.

"You know who he looks like, right? That sailor guy. Corey somebody? One of that team we saw on TV a few weeks ago?" Tayla won't let go until she's satisfied her curiosity.

"This was Sam Northcroft, the quiet one. Corey is the dark-haired, outgoing one." I busy myself in the kitchen, wiping down surfaces as tears gather in the corner of my eyes.

Tayla and I have been friends for far too long, and she notices straight away. "Hey, hey. Are you crying? Did he hurt you?" Every muscle in her body tenses up. She'd probably find out where he lives and bring back his balls in a bag if he'd hurt me physically.

"No, he was very good. VERY good." I crack a joke through my tears.

She laughs. "So it's like that, eh? Do you want to see him again?" She strokes my hair to soothe me. Daisy sits at my feet, sensing I need company.

"I do. I thought we had something special. I don't think he'll call." Tears threaten to spill over again.

Tayla tucks a strand of hair behind my ear. "You've been by my side through many fuck-ups. Now it's my turn. I decree we have a do-nothing Sunday. Watch some Netflix. Actually follow through with a skincare regime. And more importantly, takeaways for dayyyyyyssss." She blows me a kiss while sashaying away. "Let me put my pajamas on. We're in for the day, us three girls. And a big fuck you to fuckboys with ridiculous cars and small dicks."

I clear my throat.

"Fine, big dicks too." She rolls her eyes, and we laugh. For a while, it seems like everything's alright with the world again.

CHAPTER 3

SAM

a speed camera flashes on the Harbor Bridge, the main link between the northern suburbs to the town center. The tide is in, and the light winds are making the yachts bob up and down on the water's surface.

In my rush homeward, I'm speeding on the highway like I'm racing on the ocean. My pulse is up, my head feels leaden, and my thoughts are jumbled. I can't think straight. Last night is a puzzle that I can't complete, fragments of thoughts and feelings that I can't process. It's never this bad. I usually navigate through overstimulation, but this time it's different. *She* is different.

Off the bridge, it's straight into another world of older style houses and compact gardens on one side and skyscrapers on the other.

Fifteen minutes. That's how long it takes to get from my house in Bella Vista to Ellie's house. As I wait for my garage door to open, I start thinking I could turn around, fly over the bridge and be back at her house in only a quarter of an hour. That's faster than an average sailing race lap. I could go back, say all the right things, do all the right things ...

I park and enter my house through an inside door. As I stand in the hallway, I'm trying to remember why I bought this particular place. It seemed nice and cozy, a good area. Big enough for what I need, but not too big. Good entertaining, nice outdoor flow. Having come from Ellie's house, I feel like I'm in a fucking mausoleum. No laughter, no dog barking. I don't even have plants. Don't want them dying while I'm away.

I walk to my room to take a shower, and as the lukewarm water washes over my body I can't help but think of Ellie. Annoyed because I'm getting hard again at the thought of her, I dry briskly and put fresh clothes on.

The walls are trapping me in. Maybe I should go for a drive. No, I can't do that. Might end up back at her house. I pace around the open plan kitchen. I'll go for a run. It's Sunday morning. Perfect timing.

I pick up my phone and message Corey to see if he's keen to run together for an hour or so. He replies back straight away that he's up for it, and he'll see me here in ten.

If I continue pacing up and down like this, I'm probably going to tear a hole in the flooring. I decide to stand outside and look at the birds instead. Is that a tui bird call? I think I heard one this morning by Ellie's house.

Oh, for fuck's sake! I cover my face with my hands then go back inside. The scrap of paper with her number on it is where I'd left it on the kitchen counter. I'm going to have to throw it away. It's just *too* tempting.

Through the window, I see Corey's parking on the street, waving at me. I pick up my phone and keys, put on my sunglasses and cap, and give in. I pick up the piece of paper with Ellie's number and throw it in the outside bin on the way out.

"Hey, hey, bro. How's it going?" Corey's cheerful, as always, and wraps me in a bear hug. He probably wouldn't have made such a mess of everything with Ellie. Thinking of Corey with Ellie makes bile rise up my throat.

"You look a bit green, bro. Too much booze yesterday at Paddy's?" Corey's a tease. He knows me too well to think I'd drink too much.

"Nah. Let's get on with it. I say we run to the Marina, then back up the hill. Stop for a coffee on the way. How does that sound?" I'm keen for a punishing run, to make me think about anything but her, the slip of paper on top of my trash.

"Whoa. That's mean, man. We're going to be dead by the time we get back." Corey's a fitness fanatic. He's definitely joking.

"Last one buys the coffees," I throw behind my shoulder as I start running.

Corey laughs and easily catches up to me. We run in silence for the first five minutes. He keeps looking at me from time to time. He obviously wants to say something. When we stop at a traffic light, he's ready to burst. And he does. "So, what's going on? What's *really* going on?"

I lean against the pole and stretch my legs. How much should I say? What should I say? We've been sailing together for over ten years now, closer to fifteen. He knows me almost better than anyone, but I've never felt about a girl how I feel about Ellie. "Nothing."

The green man lights up, and we start running again at a steady pace. We run past tree-lined streets, wooden painted houses, and the urban landscape changes to city streets and tall apartment blocks.

A few moments later, Corey picks up the conversation like I'd not just shut it down. "Nothing like what? Is it ... a girl?" Though I'm not very good with making out the meaning behind people's inflections, even I can tell he's incredulous.

"Don't know why you're so shocked. You always see girls. I bet you weren't home last night." I poke him.

"I wasn't. Were you?" He lowers his sunglasses as if to really look at me.

Silence.

"I can't fucking believe it. Tell me everything from start to finish. Including why the fuck are we running close to twenty miles on a Sunday morning in high heat."

"You're not going to like it, Corey." It sounds like an apology, but I'm not sure why.

"I'm not going to like it because you're you, and you can't just do *casual* like the rest of us. You have to promise marriage to all of them." His words cut through me like a razor, and I retreat into silence again.

My failed engagement to Laura is still a sore point. I didn't really think we were in love, but *someone* told me friendship made a solid base for a good match. That may be true, but in our case it wasn't enough.

Corey sighs, from what feels like the depths of his soul. "I'm sorry bro. I don't want to see you hurt, that's all. Plus, what about racing? We're going away training up North starting tomorrow. Your mind needs to be focused on that, and the competitions we've got coming up. And what about the Olympics?"

He's right. He's not telling me anything I don't know. People in our position with stable relationships are few and far between. I'm happy with how my life is right now. Training. Racing. *Winning*. Proving to my parents continuously that I'm worth *something*. The last thing I'd want is *change*. Change is painful. Change is *vulnerable*.

We reach the Marina where yachts are lined up in the sun. There's hustle and bustle, families with kids eating ice creams and waiting for their turn to board dolphin safari tours. We turn around before anyone recognizes us and make our way back to my house.

The run is uphill, much more challenging, but I push on, Corey's words running through my mind. We stop at my local café for a flat white coffee. By this time I'd forgotten about our bet, whoever loses pays for coffee. I absentmindedly order two double shot flat whites and pay.

The café doubles as a roastery, selecting and roasting their own coffee beans for the best flavor. I scan the walls for art prints, and I see one I think Ellie would like with a puppy and a flower. I inwardly curse at myself for falling too hard, too fast.

"So who's this mystery girl? How did you meet?" Corey's interrogation continues. "Does she know the meme about you ... with the seagull?"

Not that again. But I laugh. "Whoever made that meme should get their ass pecked by that seagull." I shift from foot to foot. "Her name is Ellie. She's a daycare teacher."

Corey's eyebrows shoot so far up I can't help but laugh. "Mate. Mate. That's the most land-based occupation ever."

I nod, smiling sadly. Another reminder of how oceans apart Ellie and I are. "She's friends with Gracie. We met there yesterday, at the barbecue. I went to her place in Hillcrest. Came back home this morning."

The barista hands over our coffees, and we stroll back to my house instead of running. I think about the coffee Ellie made me, and more importantly what happened afterwards.

Corey keeps throwing me curious glances. "Never seen you like this, Sam. You're acting even more strangely than usual." He seems to choose his words carefully. "Not sure I like it."

"I don't like it either." It's the truth. I *don't* like feeling this way. Needy. Ready to drop everything for her.

It's only been one night. We haven't even been on a date. I

don't know her parents' names. I don't know what toppings she likes on her pizza. Does she get seasick? I do know how she lights up a room with a smile. I also know how she felt when I made her come. Her little smiles and silly jokes.

"Oh man. Will you see her again?" Sometimes I feel like Corey can see my every thought, and I hate that. We've reached my house now, and we're standing outside, coffee cups nearly empty.

"No. I didn't keep her number. It's all too messy."

Corey shakes his head, pats me on the back, and walks towards his car.

I'm surprised he's heading off so soon. "Aren't you coming in?"

"Nah, bro, I need to pack up for tomorrow. You should do the same. They pick us up around 4 AM."

"That's early. Okay, cool. See you tomorrow." I wave as he speeds off.

I have an early lunch and pack my bags for a few days away, including wetsuits and other gear. The rest of the day passes in a blur, and evening comes before I realize the sun's even begun to set.

I haven't stopped thinking about Ellie and replaying our time together in my head. In my last memory of her, she's standing in the doorway of that 50's home, waving at me as I'm leaving without saying goodbye.

The easy companionship with Laura felt like sailing on calm waters. No wind, stagnant, not really going anywhere. Being with Ellie is like a storm, like being blown away in a skiff at 50 miles an hour. Nowhere to hide, no land in sight.

I go to bed with a heavy sigh. No way I'll be able to rest. If this is my first real taste of heartbreak, then I definitely don't want any more.

SAM

The alarm wakes me up with a jolt at exactly 3:30 a.m. I've barely slept a wink, haunted by dreams of Ellie instead of my usual dreams about the ocean and calm waves. I made myself come twice, hoping to get some rest afterwards. I tried imagining other women, various celebrities, even exes. Anything. The only thing that made me come each time was remembering how good she felt in my arms.

I take a cold shower, and by the time I'm out, my phone vibrates. The guys are outside. The night air is fresh with the jacaranda fragrance filling the air. One of the guys helps me load up my gear on the bus, and I get on. A tui bird calls nearby.

The bus drives into the dark, through the inner suburbs, then on the highway up North, past the bridge, past the junction for Ellie's house, and beyond the horizon.

The guys chat about everything under the sun, from boats, to sails, to racing, until the topic turns to women. I groan inwardly. It's not even 6:00 a.m. I pretend I'm asleep to escape the chatter, but it seems they have other plans.

"Sam, we know you're awake. Have you seen that meme?"

Jake pushes his phone in my face. Bane of my existence, that fucking stupid meme. "It's a seagull, and it says Sam's new girl".

They laugh wholeheartedly. I usually love their humor, but on a day like today when I feel like death on legs, and I'm pining for Ellie, it's too much.

"Yeah, yeah. What's for breakfast?" I mumble and try to settle back down to rest. Or at least pretend I'm resting.

"How long since you last scored, Sam?" Florian, our German grinder, is quick to ask.

Corey clears his throat.

I roll my eyes and resign myself to the fact they won't leave me alone. I take a bite out of a protein bar. "Yesterday."

I'm prepared for all the guffaws and whistles. Such a team of louts. Even Jay, the gentle giant, chimes in. They all need a good dunk in cold water. I finish my protein bar, take a glug of water, and stare out the window, avoiding further conversation.

Nobody asks anymore questions, and the next two days pass in a buzz of activity, training from sunrise to sundown in all winds and weather. The mast of our ultralight carbon fiber boat stands seventy feet tall, dwarfing all other yachts in the area.

When I'm on the water I don't have time to think about Ellie. I push myself and the team harder and harder each time, and we achieve speeds that wow. Winning each time, taming and conquering the ocean.

The ocean that took Thea.

On Wednesday, the night before we're due to go back home, we all sit in a club room at the local sailing club. Some are having whisky, some are playing cards.

I'm doing both but failing miserably at cards. "Jake, how does your wife feel about you being gone all the time? How do you make it work?" The words are out of my mouth before I can take them back.

All eyes turn on me. Corey leans forward.

Perhaps Jake gives me an odd look, but I can't tell. "Give and take, mate. It's not easy. Got to prioritize. My Natalie, she's one in a million. I'm a lucky bastard." He puts down his cards.

His answer doesn't really satisfy me. How could I make it work with Ellie if I'm never around? It wouldn't be fair to her. She needs someone to be there, at least some of the time. I take another sip of whisky. It's so peaty it nearly makes my eyes water.

Jake's eyes change, in the same way Corey's eyes did when I first told him about Ellie. "Do you have a girl?"

I try to act nonchalant but can't quite make it. "Maybe."

"This girl … is she worth it?" Jake continues to stare me down.

Nobody makes a sound in the club room.

"Yes. She's one in a million, like your Nat." For the first time, I voice how I truly feel about Ellie.

"Keep her then. But when you're with us, your whole being needs to be focused on racing. No ifs, no buts. While you're at the helm, you're responsible for our lives."

I shiver at Jake's words.

Sensing the atmosphere's growing heaviness, Corey raises his glass. "Enough with the serious stuff. Sam got laid guys. By an actual woman! Wooohoo!"

Everyone bursts out laughing and singing "For he's a jolly good fellow …"

But I'm not feeling very jolly. I miss Ellie, so I slip away to my bunk where I can be alone with thoughts of her.

Corey follows me. "You need to call her. Or at least text her, Sam. It's been three days."

My smile fades. "I got rid of her phone number. I'm an asshole."

"She knows Paddy, right? Ask him. He'll know. Or at least Gracie will." Corey is full of ideas.

"I've screwed up badly, Corey. I didn't even kiss her good-bye. I ran out of there like Roadrunner chased by the coyote. I can't call her. You know what I'm like." I finally admit my shame.

"You're a prick. An ass. A barnacle. Less than a barnacle. An amoeba." Corey's running fast out of insults, and he's an inventive guy, so this comes as a surprise.

I'm mulling over an idea. "She works at a daycare. I could wait for her after work, take her for a coffee. Explain myself in person. See if she'll give me a chance. I want more than a one night stand. Maybe she does, too." My heart soars at the thought of seeing Ellie again.

Corey lifts one brow and crosses his arms. "God help you, son. You need all the luck you can get. Alright. I'm off to bed. Big day tomorrow. Long trip back."

I go to my bunk and enter straight away into the land of dreams, populated by the ocean... and Ellie.

CHAPTER 4

ELLIE

*I*n the five days since I last heard from Sam, I took Daisy out for ten walks, watched exactly four K-Dramas, three repeats of Pride and Prejudice - the BBC version - and ate two large tubs of Death by Chocolate ice cream. But who's counting?

Since Monday, I've been back to work at Cheeky Monkeys daycare, and the kids are taking up all my time. They're all sweethearts, and they challenge me in so many ways. I can't imagine my life without them.

I've secretly Googled Sam. Feeling a bit odd, learning things about him that he hasn't told me. His family, his mum and dad, his brother. His *many* competition prizes. It's like he's on a one-way mission to winning anything and everything, sailing or otherwise.

The biggest shocker of all—his failed engagement. Had to scrape my jaw off the floor. Jealousy strangled me, and I don't think it's loosened its hold ever since. I don't know how I hadn't heard of this before. He met someone and fell in love enough to propose. Doesn't match up to the Sam I've met briefly. But it's hard to really know a man you've met only once, no matter how many orgasms he gives you.

Laura Killarney is a gold medal Olympian in rowing. In the photos of them together she looks nearly as tall as him and so confident. They are much more alike than I care to admit. She's *very* good-looking, whereas I ... I'm short. I go to the gym when I remember, which is never. I don't know a thing about sailing. The list could go on.

They were engaged, then broke it off a short while before the wedding. Wouldn't be surprised if Sam left her without a word, like what he did to me.

I'm on kitchen duty today at daycare, and for a while I can afford to daydream about Sam as I prepare the kids' meals and tidy up. What's he been up to this past week? Has he thought about me at all? Gracie called on Monday to snoop. I told her Sam and I weren't suited and left it at that. She seemed quite disappointed. She prides herself on her matchmaking skills.

The clock on the kitchen wall strikes 4:00 p.m. Another day of work is coming to an end soon. I pack up the rubbish bags and carry them to the big bins outside. I'm always amazed at the amount of rubbish a small center like ours can produce, even though we're always thinking of ways to reuse and recycle.

The rubbish bins are always a pain, taller than me and too full. I sling a bag over the side of the bin and it gets stuck. I push, cringing at the smell.

"Let me help you with that."

I freeze. Can't be. But the deep, familiar voice sends tingles down my spine like only one man can do. I swivel my head around, and that very man's standing right next to the shiny black SUV. Sam Northcroft. *Damn.*

I look him up and down, incredulously. He's wearing his usual black combo of shorts, t-shirt, cap and sunglasses. He's a bit more tanned, and stubble covers his jaw and cheeks. Still makes my heart race and my mouth water. Still maddening.

"Why are you here? I'm working." My tone is short. I can't let him off the hook easily. He can't just breeze in like Prince Charming and expect me to fall at his feet after not a single word for five days, and after leaving like he left. What kind of person just shows up like this?

He takes his sunglasses off, and the dark circles under his eyes tell a grim story. "I'm sorry. I needed to see you. We could grab a drink, talk. When do you finish for the day?"

My resolve crumbles in an instant. Tayla says I'm a softie, and she's right. I'd love to see a smile on his face.

"I finish at 4:30 today. I'll see you in a little bit." I go back inside, fully aware of his blue-gray gaze boring into my back.

Over the next half an hour, I try my best not to look out the kitchen window. I didn't see him go back to his car. I didn't see him checking his phone. I didn't see him looking at the daycare entrance several times. I also didn't see him sighing, and I absolutely did not wish I could kiss him there and then ...

Deciding I'd tortured the both of us enough, I pack my bag and hastily say goodbye to a couple of the other teachers. They haven't noticed someone's waiting for me outside, and I hope to keep it that way.

When I get to Sam's car, I look through the window. He's fallen asleep, head back, auburn hair peeking from under the cap, strong arms crossed, mouth slightly open. He looks so vulnerable, so tender. I think I'm more than halfway to falling in love with him, and it's only the second time I've met him. I'm treading dangerous waters.

"Hey." I touch his arm through the open window and speak gently, trying not to startle him. He opens his eyes, realizes where he is, and jumps out to open the door on my side.

I don't make any move to get into his car, instead I take two steps towards the gate. "How about we take a walk to a place down here on the beachfront? Not far, maybe five minutes' walk."

He's unsure for a moment, then leaves his car and locks it, pulls his cap further down his face, and adjusts his sunglasses. "Let's do this." He looks like he's getting ready for battle. I'm curious why he's on edge.

We walk side by side towards the beachfront, and I wonder if he's going to try holding my hand. After how he left on Sunday, I doubt it.

"So what have you been up to?" I keep my tone light, no reproach. The implication is there, in the background. Will he take the bait though?

"I've been up North with the team, training." With the cap covering his face, and his dark sunglasses shadowing his eyes, I can't tell what he's thinking.

A family with two teen boys point at us excitedly and make their way towards us. Sam must have noticed them as well. He tenses up, his jaw sets, and he touches the small of my back. I haven't seen him like this.

An older man, probably the dad, steps forward, a star-struck grin on his face. "Sam! Sam Northcroft! You're a legend, mate. The boys want to be just like you. They've been sailing since they were five years old. Can we have a photo, please?" The dad is so excited, and I can't help but feel so happy they get to meet one of their idols.

Sam poses with them. "Well done, boys. Keep at it!" He take my hand and starts walking fast.

I can barely keep up. "Slow down, please. Your legs are longer than mine."

He relaxes slightly and walks slower, but he doesn't let go of my hand.

"This is why you weren't keen on walking, isn't it? You don't like being recognized."

"It's all part and parcel of what I do. Much easier with you around, though." He shrugs, but his words make me feel like I'm floating on a raft at speed.

ELLIE

*W*e reach the beachside bar, and he's recognized yet again. He asks for a private booth at the back, as far away from the entrance as possible, and they indulge him. I order a glass of rose wine, and he orders a ginger beer.

Only after the waitress has left, no doubt to tell everyone in the kitchen about us, does Sam take off his cap and sunglasses. His eyes are the same hue as a stormy ocean. He places a hand above mine on the table. He's got large sailor hands, rough and calloused. I shiver, remembering last weekend when his hands were all over me.

The waitress returns with our drinks, and silence hangs above us like an invisible thread.

He leans close. "I'm sorry I didn't call. I thought it was for the best." His voice is low, nearly a whisper. "I missed you." He squeezes my hand.

I try to catch a glimpse of the truth in his eyes. He holds my stare with an intensity I've seen before, when we first met. It happened only last weekend, but it feels like a lifetime.

He lifts my hand to his lips and slowly kisses it. "In the short time we've known each other, I've never seen you at a loss for words. Unlike me."

He's affecting me so much, I need to clear my head. "Is this how it's going to be? You're going to look for me when you want to get me in bed, and the rest of the time, you'll be a stranger?" I blurt out, unable to contain my feelings any longer.

He draws back, shell-shocked. I don't know what he expected but this definitely wasn't it. He's going to withdraw from me again. "I'm sorry," he mutters. "I don't know what to say. Corey would tell you all the right things, and you'd forgive him in an instant." He looks down and smiles bitterly. "He's a lucky bastard."

"I don't want Corey. I want you." And as soon as I say the words, I know them for truth. All we've got between us is one night of hot sex and one week apart, but one look in his eyes and touch of his fingers, and I know I want him.

He looks up at me with renewed hope.

"But I don't want to be messed around with. If we're dating, we're dating. If we're not dating, we're not dating." Not sure that I'm using the right words for what I'm trying to convey.

But he gets it. "We're dating. And I'll let you know in advance when I'm going away. And I'll find a way to get in touch with you." He looks serious and determined.

"Ok, let's do this." I lean over and kiss his nose. He laughs and pulls me in for a kiss on the lips.

"Shall we get food here, or …" I ask in between kissing and nibbling on his lower lip.

"How about we go to my house for dinner? I can make some sushi." He gives me a hot look while stroking my hair.

"No fucking way. You know how to make sushi?" Is there

an end to this man's skills? "Do you sing? What other talents do you have?"

He laughs heartily. "Come home with me, and I'll show you."

Now I'm really weak at the knees. We pay for our drinks and head back to his car, hand in hand.

"Where's your car? Back at the school? Do you want to follow me?" he asks all of a sudden. How thoughtful of him.

"I park down by the lake, about 15 minutes away. It's free." I raise my shoulders apologetically. "I'll leave it there tonight and bus my way in tomorrow."

He seems to think about it but doesn't say anything. We get in his spaceship of a car again, but this time he's in the driver's seat, so different from last time we were together. His hand caresses my thigh from time to time, and I feel a rush of excitement coupled with apprehension move through me. I met someone - a man I could *love*.

* * *

SAM

*W*ith Ellie by my side, the windows down, and the sea air rushing past as we drive over the bridge, I'm feeling like the luckiest man alive.

I don't know why I suggested we make sushi. I've made it once before in my life, and it was edible but not stellar. I suppose I just wanted to get her into my space, make her presence and light fill the empty corners of my house.

I'm absolutely exhausted. We trained in the morning, then started heading down to Auckland by morning teatime. After four long hours, I was back home. Showered, put on some fresh clothes, and drove straight away to the Shore to Cheeky Monkeys. And to Ellie. I feel like I've been running on a surge of adrenaline all day.

The moment I saw Ellie again I felt much she's come to mean to me in such a short period of time. It's not even been a week, and she's occupying my thoughts like no one else before her.

She's dressed in leggings and a baggy t-shirt that completely hides her figure. She could be wearing a rubbish bag and I would still want her.

We're cruising slowly on the streets of Bella Vista, the old suburb I live in. She must be taking in the surroundings because she's gone quiet. I don't think she expected that I'd live somewhere like this. When we get closer to my house, the garage door opens, and I reverse in.

"Fancy digs." She's unreadable, a mystery to me.

I pick up her hand, and lead her in through the side door, into the hallway, past the bedrooms, and into the open-plan living kitchen area.

She looks around, touches the sofa cushions, the edge of the kitchen counters. "Beautiful home you have here."

"It's from 1910. Practically ancient when it comes to New Zealand homes." My remark seems to put her at ease. "Would you like something to drink? Some more wine maybe?"

"What do you have?" She glides closer, and I show her my wine fridge.

"A wine fridge? Sam." She looks at me like I've sprouted two heads then leans down to examine the bottles.

I don't know what to say. Again. Ellie has me tongue tied. She picks out a bottle of Prosecco. "I think this one will work best with sushi."

Shit. We were going to make sushi. I totally forgot. What's in the pantry? Rice. Soy sauce. Do I have fish? Yeah, fish in the fridge. Avocado. Okay. We can make this work.

I lay everything on the counter. "Let's make some sushi then."

Ellie prepares the rice while I slice the rest of the ingredients. As the rice cools down, I show her the outside area. It's small. No big lawns, just some loungers on the deck, a BBQ in the corner, and a dipping pool.

She extricates herself from my embrace. "I just need to make a quick call to let Tayla know I'm not around."

Without her in my arms, I feel strangely bereft. I go to check on the rice.

While on the call, her eyes take in the sights in the fresh evening air, and I imagine her living here, with me. Daisy, too, of course. My yard isn't as big as the one she has now. We would have to move house, perhaps. What the hell am I thinking? Playing house with a girl I've just met. Sure, I've never felt about anyone the way I feel about her, but she's not my future, the ocean is-the Olympics, the Sanders Cup. I can't give it my all if I'm at the mercy of a woman. Settling down is a route to trouble. I can't keep these parts of my life separate. Can I?

* * *

SAM

*E*llie comes back, stands on her tiptoes, and kisses the side of my neck and jaw.

"The rice is cool enough. Now it's time to throw everything in and roll." My hands are shaking. Does she know the effect she has on me?

We roll the sushi, and I try to slice it into equal pieces, a task which at this time is as difficult to do as steering a ship through a storm. Her nearness makes it impossible to focus on anything else.

"Looks great! I'm ravenous." She picks up a piece with chopsticks and dips it in soy sauce.

I don't trust my hands to be steady enough for chopsticks this evening, so a fork it is. I stab two pieces at once and start eating.

Her eyebrows shoot up at my use of a fork, and her laughter fills the house. She tries to pinch me with the chopsticks. I put down my fork and start chasing her around the house to get the chopsticks off her.

I don't know how long it's been since I've laughed with all

my heart like this. Probably since I was a child, playing with my brother and Thea in O'Neill's Bay.

Using my larger size to advantage, I finally catch her, and we tumble onto the sofa. We start kissing with more urgency, riding waves of desire. I want to explore every inch of her, make her mine again. I can't believe I've lasted five days without hearing her voice, touching her, being in the same room as her.

She frees her dark hair from her ponytail, and it fans out onto the cushions. Tonight, I'll worship her body until she burns for me.

She takes off her oversized t-shirt, and pulls her leggings down her slim, tanned legs. I'm nearly drooling by this point. She's wearing some white plain cotton underwear that I'm dying to take off. I struggle to unclip her bra and curse my big hands. She sighs softly and helps me out. I cup her breasts, and place gentle kisses on her collarbone, the outline of her breast. Her nipples are begging for attention, so I rub my face stubble on them. She moans, and I struggle to keep a firm hold on my sanity.

Slowly, I kiss her belly, then slip her undies off, exposing her pussy. My rough stubble touching her thighs must make her feel extra sensitive. I take a first taste, she's divine. Ellie's moaning and whispering my name. I start licking and sucking her clit, and as her thighs tremble, I know she's ready to come for me. She cries out my name and comes hard.

I'm so hard, I'm ready to explode. I pick her up from the sofa and carry her in my arms to the bedroom. I place her gently on the bed, take my clothes off as I'm racing the clock, put on a condom, and slide inside her.

Ellie feels so good, like she's meant for me. Try as I might, I can't hold it in too much longer, so I claim every last bit of her.

CHAPTER 5

ELLIE

One Week Later

The box of crayons crashes with a clatter, sending its contents scattering across the floor. I stop mid-read, and the other kids all turn to the activity table, where a red-faced Oscar hides his hands behind his back.

I put down *The Very Merry Pony* and bustle towards the child, tripping on some stray LEGO blocks.

"I'm … sorry, Ellie. I'm c-c-clumsy." Oscar wipes his freckled forehead with his sleeve, his stutter returning.

I crouch down and touch his shoulders, smiling as reassuringly as I can. "It's okay, Oscar. It happens to me all the time. Isn't that right, kids?" I turn to the others, who nod at me, giggling.

Some of Oscar's tension has passed, and he's smiling back at me with a gap-toothed grin.

"Anyway, it's tidy up time. We have a VERY important guest coming today, and everything needs to look good."

I start putting away books and LEGO blocks. The other kids help Oscar put away the crayons. "Great work, kids. *Ka pai, tamariki.* Now tell me, can you guess who's coming to see us now at mat time?"

The kids shout various answers, making each other laugh. Their little individual voices blend into one loud noise.

"The Prime minister! The Queen! My mom! A potato!"

The potato guess makes me laugh just as much as them. "Some good guesses there, kids, but no. Our special guest today is a sailor for our country's national team, and he's going to tell us all about what it's like to sail on a boat."

I put a seat for myself in the corner, and all the kids hurry after me, sitting cross-legged on the mat.

I gesture to the door. "His name is Sam. Let's call out his name and see if he's ready. One, two, three ..."

Ten voices erupt into a single cry. "Saaaaaaaaam"

Sam leans into the door frame, a small smile tugging at the corner of his lips. The apprehension in his eyes is like a dam, holding his feelings in place, locking them inside a blue-gray pool.

I gesture to the seat in the middle. "Come on in, Sam. We don't bite, do we, kids?"

The kids giggle, and Sam opens his mouth to say something, thinks better of it, strides towards the chair that's clearly too small for him and squeezes his large frame into it. He waves to my preschoolers, a lopsided smile in place. "Hi, kids. How's it going?"

This looks like it's going to be a tough gig for Sam. He's fidgety, one foot already tapping. In some ways, Sam reminds me of Oscar with his short attention spans, so I try my best to put him at ease. "Tell us about yourself, Sam. What do you like about sailing?"

A small voice breaks through. "And what's your favorite shark?"

Sam leans back and starts laughing, visibly relaxing, his eyes crinkled at the corners. "Oh boy, nobody's ever asked me what my favorite shark is. Let me think. Which one's your favorite?"

Lucie shakes her blond pigtails, and her pink rimmed glasses fall down her nose. "I like Sand Tiger sharks because they have stripes, just like a real tiger. Rawr!"

Her roar catches Sam unawares, and he laughs again. The dam of wariness behind his eyes crumbles. Sam lifts his eyebrows. "That's … something. I like Hammerhead sharks. They look very cool up close."

The kids gasp in wonder."You've seen a shark up close!"

"I've seen many sharks. They had biiiiig mouths and lots of teeth." Sam shows a big mouth with his hands, and the kids gasp again.

"How did you see the sharks? Did you fall out of your boat?" Oscar's eyes are as big as saucers, and his mouth is forming a perfect O shape.

When I asked Sam last week to come meet my preschoolers at daycare, I thought I'd have to cajole him into it. He's not the most social person, and a classroom full of noisy kids is challenging for most people.

Instead, Sam surprised me by taking my hand, kissing it, and saying "*Sure,*" like I'd just asked him to watch something else on Netflix, not spend half an hour of his time with Preschool kids. "*Anything... for you,*" he'd added, still holding my hand. And I fell in love with him a little bit. Ok, maybe a little bit *more.*

His eyes sparkle while he talks animatedly about sharks, sailing, and the ocean to four year-olds, and my heart swells.

"...and when you're a bit older you can sail around the world in a boat." Sam beams at the kids, and they take in every word.

Oscar props his head with his hands, pondering something. "My grandpa told me sailors have a sweetheart in every port. Do you have a sweetheart in every port?"

Oh, shit. Oscar's grandpa and his *wisdom* is going to unsettle Sam, and it's going so well … I turn to look at Sam, but he chuckles, and shrugs. "Nah, no sweethearts."

His words are like a frozen claw squeezing my heart, and I shiver. Did he just say that? My self-esteem isn't great at the best of times, and hearing him dismiss any relationship between us, even if it's just to my kids, makes me take a deep breath. To avoid a cry-fest in front of the kids, I jump out of my seat like a jack-in-the-box, a wide smile plastered on my face. "Our special guest needs to leave now because he has a busy schedule, and it's lunch time."

Sam gets up from the too-small chair and stretches his long limbs. "See you later, kids. Be kind to your teacher." He winks at them and looks sorry to go. A sad smile tugs at the corner of his lips.

Chloe's messy bun pops from behind the door. "Ellie, you show our guest out, I'll help the kids with their lunch boxes." Chloe floats through the door in a wave of incense and flowery fabric, winking at me as she passes. She waves at Sam from a distance, and he waves back with a bemused expression, one eyebrow arched.

Sam and I walk in silence out the classroom door. We're side by side, and I'm imagining the worst possible scenarios, like is this his very unconventional way of telling me we're over? I steal glances at his profile, and he's so calm and collected, like he's got his outside mask on again.

We reach the front step of the center, and he turns to me. "How was it?"

I scan his features for any inkling of what's coming next. After all, this wouldn't be the strangest place I have been dumped. "It went well, the kids really like you."

He smiles and leans on the wall, blocking the sunshine, his shape silhouetted in the daylight. "What about you?"

Here it goes. I'm becoming belligerent, and my hands

move to my hips like they do when I'm ready for a fight. "What about me?"

He doesn't flinch or move. "Do *you* like me?"

The air from my lungs rushes out and my hands fall to my side. "Of course, I ... like you." I shield my eyes with my hand. "You're going to laugh about this."

"Oh?" Sam is still in arm's reach, so close, yet so far away.

A mortified laugh escapes me. "I thought ... because you told Oscar you have no sweethearts ... that you were going to leave me."

Sam's eyebrows shoot up. "Me? Leave you?"

"I told you you're going to laugh about this ... anyway ..." I tuck a loose strand of hair behind my ear and examine my Birkenstocks like they're the most important thing in the world because I don't dare look him in the eye.

He leans in, and his scent slams my senses like an ocean riptide. "No sweethearts. Only one. *You.*"

CHAPTER 6

ELLIE

A Few Weeks Later
It's late November and the weather continues to be mild. We've been dating for a couple of months now, and I have a day off work this Wednesday. Sam will bring Corey round to mine and Tayla's in the evening. We'll have some dinner and drinks, and we'll have each other's measure, I'm sure.

I'm a bit worried, as I have an inkling Corey might not be my number one fan. Tayla hasn't really crossed paths with Sam since that first night, when she implied he may have a small dick. I have a good laugh at the memory.

Tayla's at work today, visiting schools in her educational psychologist role, and she'll be back around 5:00 p.m.

I walk Daisy around the neighborhood, then lead her home and go out again to pick up some groceries to prepare dinner. I'm going to make a large lasagna for everyone to share with some garlic bread and salad. The boys are in charge of drinks tonight.

I'm so excited to see Sam, I've missed him over the past couple of days.

As I'm waiting for the checkout operator to process my items, my attention is drawn to the flat screen TV in the corner.A picture of a sailing boat, the NZ logo on it flashes across the screen. I squint to see the scrolling text at the bottom of the screen. "Can you turn up the volume?" I ask. The operator does and the news reporter's voice floats into the air with urgent tones. "We have breaking news. Earlier today, the New Zealand team capsized while training on the Auckland Waitemata harbor."

I register the TV presenter's words through a fog. I'm fixated by the images showing this huge boat tipped nose down in the water, some of the sailors bobbing along on the surface, boat debris floating, and my Sam, and Corey, hanging on for dear life at the back end of the boat sticking up 30 feet in the air.

"$70.25 please." The girl looks at me as if I'm crazy. I wave my card for contactless payment, pick up my bags, and run to my car. I dial Sam's number repeatedly, only to be greeted by voicemail. I send him a brief message:

"Please let me know you're ok."

I'm sobbing and shaking inconsolably in my car. I could drive down to the dock. Or maybe he's in hospital, but which one? I could start calling all of them, but I'm not next of kin. The phone's vibration jolts me, and I answer without checking who it is. Tayla's concerned voice echoes.

"Babe, I saw the news. Is everything alright?"

I let out an uncontrollable sob. "I don't know, he's not answering. He looked hurt."

"Where are you? Do you need me to come home early?" Tayla is such a good friend. Her voice soothes me.

"I'm at the supermarket. In my car. I'd bought everything for dinner, and then I saw the news. I feel foolish." I'm crying so hard, I'm hiccupping.

"You're not foolish. It's normal to care about him. Go

66

home now and keep the phone line clear in case there's news. I'll message you later on. Let me know if you need me back home."

I quickly end the call and make my way home as fast as I can. My phone remains silent, and nerves dance in my belly for the rest of the afternoon.

* * *

SAM

*I*t was supposed to be just an ordinary training day in the lead up to the Sanders Cup races next year in December. The wind gusted at about 12 knots, not too fast, not too slow. The guys were pumped after we tried, and succeeded, some tricky maneuvers around the expected course.

I steered sharply to round a corner on the home straight, thinking that in only a couple of hours I could see Ellie again. My steering took Corey by surprise, and he lost control of the sails in a gust of strong wind.

As the boat nosedived into the ocean, sending Florian, Jake, Matt and Jay crashing into the waves, several thoughts careened through my head.

They say that when you're close to death, your whole life flashes before you. I haven't lived that long, and I have so much more left to do and see in this whole wide world.

I thought of Thea, and how we played as children in the waves. I thought of what she could have become. She was always the better swimmer between us.

I thought of Ellie, and my heart ached. I can't imagine my life without her in it.

I thought of my parents, and how would they feel to lose another child.

I thought of Corey and the boys. If by a miracle we survive this unscathed, what's it going to do to the boat? It's surely ruined. Our hopes of competing next year may be dashed.

The stronger wind tipped the boat on its side, leaving Corey and I suspended 30 feet in the air, surf thundering around us.

I'm dangling in a precarious position. Should I just jump in the ocean? There is so much debris, carbon fibre, and boat equipment … I might knock myself unconscious.

The shore team is radio-ing everyone in. Eight voices reply. Relief washes over me like a gentle wave. We're going to get out of this one alive.

A rescue crew is gathering up everyone stranded, and they gently winch our boat back on its hull. Corey and I jump straight out to inspect the damage.

* * *

COREY DOESN'T SAY a word to me on the way in, and keeps his silence in the medical bay, too. Scrapes and bruises is the general verdict, and we all look a bit worse for wear. My right hand feels raw from holding on so tightly, so I have it bandaged.

"Boys, what happened out there?" Coach tries to coax an answer out of us. Corey looks out the window.

I square my shoulders. "I dropped the ball. Steered too strongly in the jibe. Sails couldn't keep up."

"You almost fucking killed us, that's what you did." Corey nearly screams at me, his face red with fury. I don't think I've ever seen him so intense. He runs his hands through his wet hair. "And you broke the fucking boat. Millions of dollars down the pan."

Coach jumps between us, holding out his palms as if he's ready to break up a fight. "Hey. Hey. It was a mistake. Not like you never make mistakes, Corey. We'll fix the boat, and have it ready to WIN by next year." He points at us. "You need to fix your friendship." He leaves us in the medical bay, and it looks like our friendship, just like the boat, may need more than a sticking plaster.

Corey gets up from his chair by the window, and walks towards me." Your mind wandered elsewhere. Don't think I haven't noticed your stupid smile when steering. You're not keeping your eyes on the horizon."

"I'm sorry. I was thinking about something else. It won't happen again." It's too dangerous to think about Ellie when the lives of seven men depend on me.

Corey stands close now, and I can see the beginnings of a scar on his cheek. He's not going to be happy about that.

"Man. Bro. Listen to me. How long have we been sailing together? Fifteen years?"

I nod. It feels like a lifetime.

"You and I, we're married to *the sea*. We go away, we come back, and that's how it's always going to be. Let Ellie make a life with someone who's going to be around for her."

Corey sure does have a way with words. Probably should have been a lawyer. The prick.

"I can't." The simple truth on my face stops him in his tracks.

"We're supposed to go to her place for dinner tonight, so you guys can meet, remember?" Feels like eons since we made these plans last week. Today I've probably aged a few years and sprouted some gray hairs.

Corey shakes his head. "Are you crazy? We just had an accident. Your fault." His eyes narrow. "Mostly."

"We don't have to do anything. Just turn up with some wine and hold a conversation. You are able to do that, I think." I can't believe I'm managing to crack jokes after being one step away from drowning.

"Man, making nice with your distraction of a girlfriend and her flatmate is the last thing I want to do right now. But I promised. I keep my promises." With one final fiery glare, Corey leaves me alone.

* * *

BACK AT MY LOCKER, I turn my phone on, and I'm greeted with a deluge of missed calls, voicemails and messages. Oh shit. The boat capsize must have made the news. I bet everyone is worried sick.

I call mum, assure her I'm okay and that I'm definitely coming down for Christmas. I message everyone else, from my brother to Paddy.

I leave the most important call until last. Ellie's voice is trembling.

Instantly, I feel the need to see her, hold her, tell her everything will be fine. "Hey you. I'm sorry I couldn't answer sooner … I'm okay, could be worse … Are we still on for tonight? Yes, we're both coming. See you soon."

After I hang up, I get ready to face the media. They'll have a million questions about what happened and what caused it. I just need to hold on while the storm rages.

CHAPTER 7

ELLIE

I lay, a sobbing blob in the middle of the couch, my arms wrapped around a sympathetic Daisy. Knowing he's okay, knowing he'll be here soon ... it doesn't seem to matter. Seeing him on the five o'clock news, bruised and battered, broke my heart into tiny pieces, and I don't seem to be able to glue those pieces back together.

Tayla lounges in a nearby armchair. "Why couldn't you have found a yoga teacher? Or a chess player? Or a real estate agent?" Even through my shocked state she manages to cheer me up. "Anyway, we'll see what condition they're in when they walk through that door. I can't believe they're still coming, to be honest."

After I got Sam's call earlier, I started frantically preparing the dinner in advance. Everything was ready. It just needed to be reheated.

I see Tayla's made an effort, wearing a colorful strappy summer dress, showing off her tan and pink hair. I wonder what Corey will think of her. More importantly, I wonder what Corey will think of me. I've decided to stay casual in some denim shorts and a loose blouse.

The Spaceship pulls into our driveway. The boys get out of the car and walk towards our front door.

Corey is only just slightly shorter than Sam with dark hair and sharp features. He's wearing a short sleeve shirt, shorts, and flip flops. He's taking in the street and houses with a wistful look. Daisy lets out a friendly bark.

I can't wait for them to knock, so I open the door as they're climbing the front stairs. The sight floors me. I saw them earlier on the news, and I thought I'd be prepared for the extent of their injuries, but this is something else. My heart aches just looking at them.

My Sam's right hand is bandaged. He's trying to cover his arm by wearing a long sleeve shirt. He's got a cut across his left eyebrow. His eyes are feverish, maybe from exhaustion, adrenaline, or both.

Corey has a mark on his left cheek, like he's just been on the losing end in a fight. More so, the dynamic between the two men is strange. They're refusing to look at each other. Corey's hands-in-pockets stance and lack of smile makes me think I'm dealing with some of the toddlers at the daycare, not some thirty something year old men.

Tayla steps forwards with purpose. "You guys look like you've come straight from a boxing match."

Corey picks up the gauntlet. "Sea punched us good today. I'm up for a rematch." Daisy goes straight to him and wags her tail. He pats her on her back, gives her a few rubs, and she sighs contentedly. It looks like he's made another conquest.

I hug Sam hard. There are no words to express what I feel right now. The couple of hours when he was out of reach have been hell. His lips touch my forehead, then he kisses me slow and sensuously on the lips. Feels like time stands still, and it's just him and I for a short while.

Corey clears his throat pointedly.

Sam pulls away from our kiss, a smug grin on his lips. "Ladies, this is Corey. Corey, this is Ellie and her flatmate Tayla." Sam makes the introductions without breaking eye contact with me.

I slip out of Sam's embrace and shake Corey's hand. Tayla, a shade braver than me, kisses him on the cheek.

Tayla gestures towards the empty wine glasses. "Don't let the wine warm up, will you? We're parched."

Corey takes a hint and pours just the right amount of the New Zealand Pinot Noir.

I step away from the group and toward the back deck. "Let's eat outside. More room to breathe. It's such a nice evening." I lead them to our deck table, which is much more spacious than our kitchen table. We spent ages choosing the right tableware and serviettes to go with the occasion. But the sight that opens before us is perfectly curated to set the right mood.

I'm really proud of our outdoor space. It's only a rental property, but Tayla and I have put our heart and soul into this place. We have an avocado tree, which is great because we're both avo fiends. In one corner we keep some seasonal flowers, but it's mostly a veggie garden. Saves on costs, and it's good for the environment.

Corey looks around with an impenetrable smile. "I was telling Sam on the way here, this area, and this sort of house, reminds me of my nana's house up North."

Sam picks up my hand and kisses it. "Ellie is from up North."

"I wouldn't go as far as to say that. Matakana is still in Auckland."

They all burst out laughing at my quip, but it's all in good spirit. I'm used to this type of reaction, because even though Matakana is over an hour away from Central Auckland, it's still part of the greater Auckland area.

"So you're a country girl." Corey takes a sip out of his glass of red wine.

"Nah, not so much. I grew up in Auckland, then my parents bought up there, and we moved when I turned fourteen. I moved back for university."

Tayla senses I'm getting uncomfortable, and she intervenes. "And that's where we met!"

Corey's attention moves to her, which I'm thankful for. Sam continues stroking and kissing my hand from time to time, as if to show support.

Corey lifts his chin in Tayla's direction. "What's your story?"

Tayla puts her drink down, clearly interested in his question. "My story? I'm from Christchurch originally, but then I moved to Dunedin with my aunt. I came to Auckland for university and never left. Ellie and I studied child psychology together, but we chose different career paths. She's a daycare teacher, I'm an educational psychologist visiting various schools across Auckland."

Corey looks suitably impressed.

Now's my cue. "You guys must be starving after such an eventful day. Let's eat!" I get up and turn down Sam's offer of help because his right hand is bandaged up. Tayla joins me, and we leave the boys behind, while we pick up the goods from the kitchen. Daisy stays behind by Sam and Corey's side, like the traitor she is.

"So, what do you think?" I quiz Tayla as soon as we're out of earshot.

"Your guy ... he's not much of a talker, is he?" We both laugh because she couldn't be more true. Sam isn't a man of many words, which is why it's always odd seeing him on TV or watching old interviews.

"No, he isn't. He's a man of action." We laugh again. It could be the wine, or just the relief that they made it out alive. "What about Corey? I think we've made a good impression so far, and by we I mean you."

Tayla seems to find this hilarious. She's always had bad luck with guys. They've mostly been players or just not ready to commit to a stable relationship, which is what I think she'd be into.

"Let's go back before they send a search and rescue party for us." I pick up the lasagna, and Tayla juggles the salad bowl and garlic bread.

The moment we step outside I sense a change in mood. It's gone from lively to below freezing. Sam's jaw is set in angry lines, and Corey has a mutinous look about him, keeping his arms crossed as if to keep the world at bay. Even Daisy is unsettled, moving between the men, whining softly. If I didn't know better, I would have thought they were two toddlers arguing. Again.

Oh boy. Tayla and I exchange glances. What happened? What could they have possibly argued about after everything seemed to go so smoothly?

We place the food on the table, and I try to sound cheerful. "Bon appetit! Serve yourself. Have as much as you like."

Corey goes first and puts a chunk of lasagna on his plate, changes his mind, and adds a bit more.

I help Sam, aware of his bandaged right hand.

We eat in silence for a short while, but Tayla's brow furrows by the minute, and I think she's about to implode.

She takes a sip of her wine and grabs the bull by the horns. "So, what did you guys talk about, while we were getting the food? It seems like you're in a bad mood."

Sam finishes chewing, swallows and takes a sip of his wine. Corey looks into the distance, as if he's wishing to be as far away from this place as possible.

But Sam's right here, right now, and he's furious. "Corey

was talking shit, yet again, about my relationship with Ellie. I won't have it, more so not in your house."

Sam's words make me feel small. Corey is such an important part of his life. Most weeks he sees him more than me. On one hand, I would hate to be the reason he'd lose a friend and sailing partner. On the other hand, what if Corey's planting doubts in Sam's mind about me, about us?

Tayla looks Corey straight in the eye, leveling a challenge. "Well mate, you can fuck right off. You don't come to our house, eat our food, and dick us about with your I'm-better-than-you attitude."

Corey seems to realize he's been out of line, rubbing his chin and gazing downwards. "Sorry, ladies. I've had a very difficult day, and I'm still sore. Probably best to go home and have a rest. We have a big day again tomorrow. The food's really delicious, though." He gets up from the table.

Sam gets up with him, shaking his head at his friend.

We walk to the door, and I'm still shell-shocked by what happened. It was supposed to be the start of a great friendship, at least that's what I'd imagined. Now it's painfully obvious Corey wants me out of Sam's life.

Sam sidles up next to me and pulls me around the corner, away from everyone. "I'm his ride, but I don't have to be. I'll tell him to call an Uber."

It's tempting. Knowing what Corey thinks about me, I don't want Sam cozied up with the other man for any amount of time. But I won't put a further rift between them. That certainly wouldn't win him over. "No. It's okay. Take him home. Try to mend things. If you can." I kiss him on the cheek, squeeze him tight. "I'll see you later."

Sam embraces me and kisses me again, only for the second time tonight. He whispers in my ear, "I'm sorry. I can't stay tonight. More training early in the morning. We'll speak tomorrow, then I'll see you on Saturday. We need to plan something nice together."

As Sam's car pulls away from our driveway, I blow him a kiss, and he smiles back at me. I wonder if Corey will succeed at breaking us apart, or will we go the distance. A shiver runs right through me, and I close the front door, and help Tayla tidy up.

CHAPTER 8

ELLIE

By the time Saturday morning comes around, I haven't seen Sam for a few days, but it feels like an eternity. The more he goes away, the more I miss him. I guess that's the curse of the one left behind. He goes away on his adventures at sea, and I always stay back. A bit like moving to Matakana in the country, and all my friends staying behind in the hustle and bustle of Auckland. I'm also terrified about him thinking I'm too needy. A hot sports star's needy girlfriend. Sounds ... frightening. In his shoes, I'd run a mile.

In school I learned about the myth of Odysseus and Penelope, and how she weaved when he was away, and I thought to myself, how ridiculous. why would she wait for him? Now I can see why. *Love*. Penelope loved Odysseus so much, she waited for him. I wonder if I'm strong enough to do the same.

I've kept our relationship quiet so far. Tayla is the only one in my tight knit circle who knows I'm dating Sam. I haven't even told my parents yet that I'm seeing somebody. It's only been a couple of months, but with Christmas in a few weeks, I'm curious what will happen. Will Sam visit his family, and I'll visit mine, and then we'll see each other at New Year's?

Sam told me to get ready for a hike and swim today, so I'm wearing a two-piece swimsuit under shorts, a tank top, sneakers, and a whole heap of sunscreen. I have no inkling of where he wants to take us today. Tayla thinks it's one of the West Coast beaches, with their wild untamed beauty. Unfortunately, the area is off limits for dogs because the native birds sett up their nests there, so my sweet Daisy stays behind today.

Sam's car pulls into our driveway, and I slip away before Daisy wakes up the whole neighborhood. I get into his car, drop my backpack, and lean in for a kiss. In a second our kiss deepens, and it feels like his hands touch as much of me as they can. I've missed him so much. I sigh and lean back in my seat.

He takes hold of my hand. "I missed you."

"I missed you too. Glad to see your hand is better." I trail kisses on his hand and calloused palm. "Where are we going today?"

He takes off his sunglasses and looks at me with the heat of a thousand suns. That smile of his lights up my day. "You'll have to wait and see."

We're on our way, and I take the time to really look at him. He's still the same Sam, scruffy cropped auburn hair and five o'clock stubble. He's dressed all in black—shorts, t-shirt, cap and sneakers. We haven't talked about what happened with Corey since that disastrous dinner on Wednesday, and I know they went sailing together on Thursday and Friday while the boat was being fixed.

"How's Corey?" I ask, unable not to. I place a hand on Sam's leg, as if to remind myself I'm indeed *not* jealous of the guy who's known him for longer and spends much more time with him. Oh, and hates my guts for some reason or another.

"He's well. Had a good time training together. No news really."

Sam delivers the information so evenly, without an ounce of emotion, that I'm left with so many questions. Did they reach a truce? Did Corey succeed in changing his mind, making him care less? I don't detect any change in his demeanor towards me, so I guess it's good news for me. I don't want to battle with Corey. He's such a big part of Sam's life that we need to get on if Sam and I are going to make this work. Important as it is, though, I don't want to think about how to get closer to Corey right now.

Sam starts the journey out West. Tayla was right. She'll be pleased when she finds out.

We make small talk about my work, his team, what the weather has in store for us, then he makes a sharp turn down an unsealed road.

"Gosh, thank goodness we're in your car. My car wouldn't have made it one mile down this road," I joke as pebbles and dust rise around us, almost completely obliterating visibility.

Sam looks so calm and collected, like he's gliding on water. We reach the end of the road, and I see a walkway through the native rainforest. Large ferns, Cabbage trees, and giant Kauri trees over twenty-five feet tall, loom over us.

We grab our backpacks and leave the car behind. This trail is unfamiliar to me, but I don't feel any fear walking by Sam's side. As we walk, we listen for bird calls local to New Zealand. It's cool but humid under the vast canopy. Sam moves with ease, his long limbs stepping over rocks and logs. I struggle a bit, but his steadying hand is always there to help me.

We stop a few times and take a few selfies.

"I want to put a photo of you on my Instagram." His face is unreadable. His new determination to create memories together surprises me, but also makes me feel cherished.

"Are you sure it's a good idea? People will talk."

He shows me his phone. "Pick a photo. Or however many you want."

I scroll through the photos and choose one of both of us walking side by side through the rainforest, grinning ear to ear.

"Post this one. If anyone asks, you can say I'm your personal trainer."

He laughs so much I think he'll explode. I'm much shorter than he is and definitely not a fitness icon. My Instagram account is mainly photos of Daisy, my garden, and landscapes. I have a total of 15 followers, counting Tayla.

He elbows my arm. "Nah, you're alright." He posts the photo of us on his personal account, and though I'm dying of curiosity, I'll wait until later to see what mayhem he's unleashed. With some luck, it will be glossed over. After all, people shouldn't be interested in his love life. They should care about his sailing performance, right?

Keeping my fingers crossed behind my back for that one, we push onwards hand in hand.

Until I hear a distant sound. "A waterfall!" I'm giddy with excitement. "I love waterfalls so much. How did you know?"

He looks very pleased. "I had no idea. Just thought it would be a good place I could take you."

Another five minutes' walk, and we've reached the base of the waterfall. It's one of the most beautiful sights I've ever seen in my life. Water cascades through three ledges and plunges into a clear blue pool below. Drops of water shimmer like jewels in the sun. I take a couple of photos, but I can't do it justice.

Sam puts his hand on my back, and I turn to face him.

The sun frames him, and his hair glints in the light like russet fall leaves with golden hues. He takes his sunglasses off, and a storm is brewing in his eyes the color of the deep ocean. Without giving me a chance to catch a breath, he pulls me closer, until I'm immersed in the eye of the storm.

"I missed you." Sam's whisper, so close to my lips, makes me tingle from the top of my head to the tip of my toes. Our lips meet with a hunger I've never felt before. For any man.

Sam lifts me onto a grass slope, and we drop out backpacks with a thud on the ground. One of his hands has a firm grip on my ass, while the other hand does wicked things to my breast. I can feel his hardness through his shorts, and I know he's burning for me. The idea that this is a public place, that there could be other walkers, makes me want him even more than I thought possible.

Sam pushes down my shorts and swimming briefs, pulls down his own shorts, slides inside me with a moan, and moves with urgency. I've missed the feeling of him. It's like there's an emptiness in me only he can fill. His whole body tenses, and he comes deep inside me, sending me right over the edge.

We hear voices in the distance, and he gently takes me down off the grassy slope, pulls his clothes up, and helps me lift my clothes. We grab our backpacks and slip away unnoticed.

"I have something else to show you." Sam takes my hand and leads me on a different path to the one we arrived on.

"Oh, you've shown me plenty." My double meaning makes him laugh. He likes feeling wanted, my Sam.

The vegetation seems sparser now, and I can see sand creeping in between the trees. I can hear waves crashing in the background. He's taking me to the beach for a swim.

* * *

SAM

I didn't know how I'd feel seeing Ellie again after that shocker of a dinner on Wednesday night. I wasn't prepared for the strength of my feelings for her. I've never believed that absence makes the heart grow fonder, on the contrary. I think it dulls feelings. Or I used to think that until I met and fell hard for Ellie.

It's scary how one day you're your own person, and what feels like the next day, your whole world revolves around another individual. I absorb all her gestures, little smiles, and touches. I still can't read her body language well, but with her, I'm the closest I've ever been to succeeding.

I could tell she was surprised by my Instagram idea. I only hope I'm not throwing her to the wolves. I'm going to protect her as much as I can.

Now we walk hand in hand on the black sand beach, waves thundering in the distance, and no lifeguard in sight. Many people avoid West coast beaches because they're notoriously wild. Adrenaline junkies like me love them because of it.

I brought Ellie here because it's a part of me, one that she doesn't get to see, reckless, wild and carefree. I set down my backpack, take out a towel, take off my shoes and shirt, and leave my cap and sunglasses behind. Ellie takes off her clothes, revealing a two-piece swimsuit. She's small but curvy in all the right places.

I smack her ass playfully. "Last one in the water is a loser." I sprint for the surf, and she trails behind me, laughing. I win of course, and crash into a wave, letting out a cheer. I surface and look for Ellie. She is farther away from me than I would like and moving even further by the second. The water she's wading in looks calm, but the speed she's traveling away from me sounds alarm bells in my head. She's in danger.

"Ellie, darling, don't panic, okay. You're in a rip now. Just relax and try to float. Once you're out of the rip, you can swim sideways towards me." I hope my voice is soothing enough because inside I'm screaming.

Fear gathers in her widening eyes. "Sam." Her voice is choked with panic. "I can't feel the seafloor. I'm scared, Sam. Help me." Her plea rips me to shreds. If we go together in the rip, there's no guarantee we'll make it. I look around frantically for a lifeguard but see no one.

A wave washes over her, and she's under.

"Ellie!" I scream and dive in, through the rip, to where she was just a second earlier. My only thought is I need to find her, I need to save her. The water is silty which is unhelpful, and the visibility is poor. I can barely see two feet ahead, so I flail my arms, hoping to touch Ellie. Panic threatens to claim my self control, and I struggle to stay calm. Panicking requires more air, and my lungs hurt already from the pressure. I can't give up. Not now.

My fingers feel something solid, and before joy overtakes me, I lift Ellie up and out of the water. We take a big gulp of air. Her eyes are open, but she feels heavy in my embrace, limp from exhaustion. I work hard to keep us both afloat as the rip carries us towards the deep. It's only a couple of minutes, but it feels like hours. I draw upon my training in yachting, capsizing, mindfulness, and everything else I can think of to stay strong and get her to shore. When my feet hit the seafloor, I can finally fully breathe, finally hope.

We collapse on the sand and spend several moments trying to get our breath back, chests heaving. As soon as I'm able, I get up and inspect every inch of Ellie. Will I have to call an ambulance?

She looks at me with her soft brown eyes and grabs my hand. "You've saved my life, Sam. Oh my. Out there, I thought it was the end."

This is all too much. I stand up and pace away. The unfamiliar feeling of tears burns my eyes. This time, I saved her. What if I lost Ellie?

Like I lost Thea.

Ellie wraps her arms around me. I hug her tightly, like I don't want to ever let go.

Her teeth are chattering. "Shall we go back? I'm cold."

I kiss her again, we towel down, dress, and walk back, slower this time, past the massive Kauri trees, past the waterfall where we made love, and past the places where we took photos.

It's close to lunchtime, and I'm starting to think about the rest of the day. Driving back towards the Shore, I get an idea.

"Why don't I drive you home, you pick up some clothes and Daisy, and come to mine for the rest of today and tomorrow? I can drop you off home Sunday night." Fuck. We nearly drowned. I nearly lost her, and I refuse let her go, even if it's to a different part of town.

She's never stayed the weekend before, and after making

it Instagram official, this is a big move. It means something for us, and she knows it. She must, the way she's chewing her lip and eyeing me. Is she unsure? "Please?" My fingers twine with hers, handing my heart over completely.

CHAPTER 9

ELLIE

y phone sits like a snake on the edge of Sam's kitchen table where it's been since I got here last night. I haven't touched it. Turned it to silent, not wanting to know what awaited me—silence or chaos?

But it's time. I can't avoid it, the world, forever. I reach out, my hand quick as lightning, and I grab the phone, turning it over and on at the same time. Twelve missed calls, fifteen messages, and two hundred notifications from Instagram. Shit. Shit shit shit. "Shit."

"Something wrong?" Sam's voice floats in from the living room.

Color me surprised. My fifteen followers on Instagram has morphed into 3,000. I check my direct messages. A quick scroll through shows most of them are from shady weight loss businesses asking to collaborate. They're all from yesterday, right after Sam brought me out of obscurity by announcing he was having a great time outdoors with me and tagging me in that photo.

One of the few texts I actually open and read is from Tayla, who messaged me almost immediately after Sam posted the picture. Stalker. She sent a screenshot and a few pointed question marks. I reply, "Yeah ..." then slam the phone face down on the table. There's nothing else to tell her, really. It's quite straightforward. We're Instagram official. Luckily my parents don't have Instagram, so I have a few days left with them—maybe more if I can stretch it—before I have to explain what's going on.

I ignore my phone and focus on the omelettes I'm making for a hearty lunch. "Ready!" I call, and Sam joins me. My phone winks at me like some malicious demon from the tabletop, and I move it to the counter.

Sam's phone buzzes all through lunch, but he seems unconcerned. His phone keeps buzzing, but he continues to ignore it.

He ignores it after lunch, too, and while we order takeout for dinner. He ignores the buzzing, still, as we choose a movie to watch - The Avengers.

The buzzing is like my own personal hell. I break. "I don't want to pry, but aren't you going to answer your phone? Could be something important."

He looks at me like it's a mad suggestion. But he picks up his phone, scrolls through it, then puts it down with a sigh. "Corey. And Mom."

I'm shocked that he could be so blasé about this. "Flick them a call. Could be something serious. It's important, Sam."

"Sit with me," he implores. Daisy and I curl on the sofa next to him. He makes the first phone call.

"Hey mate. Nah, all good ... I wanted to show her off a bit." Sam winks at me, and I laugh. "See you on Monday back at the dock." He ends that call and gets ready for the one he seems the most uncertain about. His mum.

"Hey mom, it's Sam." He listens intently as his mother chatters away at length. His brow furrows. "She is special ... No, she doesn't know." I hear his mum mention the name

Thea, but it doesn't mean anything to me. I thought his ex's name was Laura. Maybe I was mistaken. "I'll ask her." He covers the mobile speaker with his hand.

"I know it's a bit left field, but with Christmas around the corner, mum wants to know if you're coming down to theirs with me." I try hard to read his expression. Does he want me to go with him? Is he just trying to be polite?

"You don't have to say yes."

I figure I have nothing to lose by accepting. It could offer me another glimpse into the Sam enigma. "Happy to come with you. We'll talk about preparations later." Hope I've put him at ease.

He nods and puts the phone back to his ear. "We're coming together. Yes, we can stay in my old room. Don't want to be any bother. We'll talk later. Don't worry, it's all fine." As soon as he's ended the call, he relaxes. I don't know what sort of relationship he has with his parents, but it looks like waters run deep.

I rest my head on his shoulder, and we start kissing again in the afternoon sun. Tui birds call outside, disturbing Daisy from her rest.

SAM

I don't take girls to my parents' home as a rule. There's always an exception to the rule, and that was Laura, but we were already engaged when I mustered the courage to take her back home to O'Neills Bay. We stayed in an Airbnb, went to my parents' for lunch, and that was that.

My mum and dad seemed to genuinely like her, but after we broke up three years ago mum had some choice words for me. "You're wasting your life, Sam. Why can't you find a nice girl like your brother Tom did? One with an actual job? Settle down and stop gallivanting around the world. You're pushing 30. I want grandchildren."

She was being deeply unfair to Laura, who's an Olympic rowing champion. That's definitely a *job*.

But Mum also doesn't think what I do is a job. She's right on one account. It's more than a job. It's a passion. Nobody gets to Olympic level without hard graft, but the secret ingredient is passion.

Laura and I didn't work out, but mum kept the bee in her bonnet about me abandoning sailing and racing and settling down in a "real job". This is why I don't visit her and dad as often as I should. The last thing I need is to get an earful about how dangerous it is, about how it can all disappear in an instant.

She called today because the daughter of one of the other nurses at the children's hospital in O'Neill's Bay told her mum, who in turn told *my mum* there's a girl on my Instagram. Typical, small town grapevine. I never post truly personal stuff, so it was a like posting a neon sign over my head.

The news has likely already gone round the supermarket, the boat club, the Crab Shack café, and the local bank branch. I'd be surprised if the carers in the nursing home haven't told my Nana about it yet. My dad, who's oblivious to most things, will have been told on some building site or another. Tom may be Mum's golden boy, but I feel golden with Ellie by my side. I'm ready to show her off, and what better way than at Christmas.

"About Christmas. I know it's also your birthday, but you kept that one quiet." Her words bring me back to reality with a thud the next day. I run my hand through my hair.

"I don't really celebrate. How did you find out?" I'm starting to feel uneasy. What else has she found out? Like a dog with a bone, my mum rang straight away to push to meet Ellie. One of the first things she asked me was whether Ellie knows about Thea.

She laughs. "I Googled you after we met."

I try to keep a neutral tone, but I'm nervous. "And what did you find out?"

"Nothing to scare me off. Yet." She thinks she's hilarious.

I haven't talked to anyone apart from Corey and Jay about what happened. It's something that will stay with me forever. I'm scared that once Ellie finds out, she'll see me in a different light … and leave. "Good." I kiss her forehead and pull her closer. She must have read about Laura and decided it wasn't a big deal. Perfect. It wasn't.

"Tayla is away at Christmas. I'll take Daisy to my parents' place in Matakana for the holidays, then on Christmas morning we can go to yours."

Is she inviting me to meet her parents? I can't tell. "If you want me to meet your parents before you meet mine, that's fine."

She nods, a little smile tugging at her lips. "How about we drive Miss Daisy there on Christmas Eve, have dinner with my parents, exchange presents, then on Christmas morning make our way to O'Neill's Bay?"

This approach makes more sense to me. I'm intrigued to meet her parents and learn what makes her tick. "Driving Miss Daisy, eh?" I like her goofy sense of humor. "We could take her to O'Neill's Bay, but it's a long drive. If your parents are happy to have her for a couple of nights, we can fetch her back on the 27th."

She relaxes against me, her muscles turning to liquid with each pull of my fingers against her scalp. But I can't relax. I stay as tense as the rope connecting an anchor to a boat. I'll get to show her off at Christmas, but what will she learn about me? About Thea? And more importantly, how will she react when she finds out?

CHAPTER 10

ELLIE

Christmas Eve

I stare at a picture of a purple cat with mile-long whiskers wearing a princess crown, but I think of Sam. The kids run around the room, impossibly excited at the coming Christmas holiday. Their cries and songs and requests blur together, and I think of Sam. There's probably a dreamy smile on my face, too.

Someone pulls at my shirt. "Ellie, can we read The Very Merry Pony again, please?" Oscar's tiny voice cuts through my thoughts. I've been daydreaming of Sam again, something I do frequently. Too frequently for my liking.

I pick up the colorful book again for the fifth time today.

Four small faces stare back at me with intent and curiosity.

"Ok, kids. This is *The Very Merry Pony*, written by a nice author called …" I check the cover again. I can't concentrate for the life of me. In just a few hours Sam will meet my parents. My heart rate is through the roof.

"Ashley Parkes," Oscar whispers loud enough for everyone in the entire center to hear.

I chuckle. "That's right, Oscar. Ashley Parkes."

Since going public with Sam on Instagram, my life has been manic. My parents found out, so I had to explain, like I'm some sort of teenager. Then all my university girlfriends wanted to know why, how, when, and how often, but I brushed them off.

A style magazine actually posted our photo together and made it into a fashion feature, with where they thought our clothes were from. They got the value of my gear wrong though, I don't wear $100 LuluLemons. I'm a Kmart girl at $10 a pair.

Somehow, I get to the end of *The Very Merry Pony*, and parents begin streaming through the door to pick their kids up early. Being Christmas Eve, there aren't many kids in today to begin with. When the excited hum of little kids voices turns to silence, and the last kid is gone, us teachers finish tidying up, then have a shared lunch. We swap secret Santa presents. I give Hamida a gorgeous scarf, and she loves it. In return I get a lush box of artisan chocolates from Chloe. Sam and I could eat them in the car on the way up to Matakana.

I drive home to pick up Daisy, get my bags, and make sure everything is closed up for a couple of days. When I drive up, Tayla's car isn't the only one in the drive, and I find my roommate and Sam's best friend on the front porch engaged in some sort of staring contest.

I put on my sunniest voice. "Hi, Corey. What brings you here?"

He's holding a huge hamper and he pushes it in my direction. "Happy Christmas. And … I'm sorry. Next time, we're doing dinner at my house." Corey winks.

He's such a charming ratbag, I think I forgave him straight away and take the basket from him.

"You're gonna need a bigger gift," Tayla snaps. "Nahhh.

Keep groveling." Her pink hair swishes. Is she ... flirting with Corey?

Corey pretends to loosen up his t-shirt collar and walks backward toward his car. "Until next time. Happy Christmas, ladies. I'm sure I'll see more of you now than ever." His car roars to life and he disappears down the road.

I raise my eyebrow at Tayla.

"What? He's hot. But he's also a ratbag. Not going to let him off the hook so easily. Anyway, I'm off to Dunedin. Gotta catch the midday flight."

I gather Daisy and my bags and bundle it all into my car then take off on the short drive to Sam's place.

I made the rather rash decision to go up to my parents in *my* car to drop Daisy, then switch to his car for the longer drive down to O'Neill's Bay. It just ... felt right. I want to show my parents I'm still *me*, regardless of who I'm dating. Famous athlete or not.

Today is the day. We leave for Christmas Eve. Not even a very merry pony can distract me from my excitement. But ... it's not all good vibes pouring through me. Doubt nags at me, too. I've barely seen Sam over the past two weeks. We've had stolen moments here and there, times when we've pulled each other's clothes off hungrily, but not enough. Every moment felt rushed, his thoughts somewhere else, likely towards the big race for the cup at the end of next year. The race is consuming him in a way I could never have imagined before. I feel like he's in a snowglobe, or perhaps a terrarium, moving around in his own world, and I'm stuck outside, looking in.

When I get to Sam's house in Bella Vista, I message him to come down. Wow, he's made an effort. For a start he's wearing shoes and socks. Some dark jeans and a nice casual shirt hug him in all the right places.

His brow is furrowed. "I don't understand how you

convinced me to go in your car. Look at it. It's held together by chewing gum and prayers."

I can't contain a laugh at that. "She's a nice little runner. I've had her for over eight years now, since I learned to drive. Surely you must remember your first car."

"I remember alright. It was a Ford Laser Sport 1987, a bit similar to this one. The only difference is mine went to the wrecker's yard, which is what yours should do, too." He knocks on the roof, and one of the side mirrors drops. I reattach it. He puts a duffel bag in the boot, gives Daisy a pat in the back seat, and gets in the passenger's seat, still shaking his head.

I stroke the dashboard. "Don't listen to him, Dorothy. You've been a very good car."

He laughs. I blast the music as loud as the old stereo will allow, and we set off northbound towards my parents' place.

The cheer is short lived, as exactly halfway to Matakana, there's smoke under the hood, and I have to pull over, to Sam's increasing annoyance.

"For fuck's sake, Ellie. This tuna can isn't even capable of making it a hundred miles up to your folks' place. We're stranded on the state highway with your dog, cars flying past doing a hundred."

Between us, he knows a bit more about engineering, and he manages to get the car to start again. We get back inside, and he's deadly serious. "You're getting a new car."

I laugh. "And you're funny. I can't afford a new car. Why do you think I drive this one?"

"I'm going to buy it for you. Consider it a Christmas present." He seems quite pleased with the thought.

"I'm sorry but I can't accept it. It's too much. I'll just get a loan from the bank and pay it off in installments." My pride is wounded. I don't earn much, but I'm proud of my work and what I've achieved so far in life. Whatever anyone else says, Olympian or not.

"How about I buy it for you, and you pay me back?" He's like Daisy with a bone. Once he has something in his sights, he doesn't let go.

"I'll think about it." I try to shrug it off, hoping against hope he forgets.

"Don't think about it. It's settled. When we come back from O'Neill's Bay, we'll look at some car dealerships." Sam leans back with a smug look on his face.

This raises my hackles faster than you can say *broken radiator*. He thinks he can hypnotize me with those eyes, and I'll just fall at his feet and do everything he asks just because?

A road sign for Matakana speeds past, and I let a deep breath out. He's meeting my parents, and it's Christmas Eve. Chill, Ellie, chill. I turn down the radio volume. The tunnel gives way to native rainforest, and native rainforest merges into vineyards on sunny hills. "Have you ever been up here?"

"I've been through here many times, but not stopped. Seems like there are a few wineries nearby. One time we should come up here and check some out, do some tastings."

I like it that he comes up with future date ideas.

I turn off the highway onto a smaller road, then when I see the all too familiar sign for Ako Wines, I turn onto the long driveway. With one eye, I spy his reaction. He seems stunned and rightly so. My parents own a small winery North of Auckland. He may have even tried their wines and not known. I park up and let Daisy out. She feels right at home among the vines.

"So, what do you think?" I try to gauge his reaction.

"I don't know what to say. Is this your parents' place?" He's standing in the courtyard, taking in his surroundings like I've taken him to outer space not outer Auckland.

"Yes. Let's leave the bags for later." I grab his hand and

lead him to the massive front door that I open without knocking.

"Anybody home?" I try to see everything through Sam's eyes. Though large, the house looks very shabby and worn. I'm sure I would ordinarily say it's a house lived in, but with fresh eyes it just looks a bit dirty and neglected. I'm suddenly nervous. Maybe bringing Sam home for Christmas Eve was not the best idea.

SAM

From the moment we turned into the Ako Wines driveway, I've been in a surreal movie with a dreamlike quality.

It's a winery. Ellie never told me her parents own a working winery. This is huge. Secondly just what the fuck is happening in this house? There are several clocks, and they all tell different times. Does my head in. I'm barely containing myself from going around and changing them all to the right time. Thirdly, I hate to say it, but it's untidy. Huge house, stuff everywhere. Makes me very anxious, like a sensory overload.

Ellie squeezes my hand. She can tell I'm uncomfortable. Her mum and dad come through a side door, and she hugs them tightly.

Her mum is crying."We missed you so much."

Ellie hugs them back just as tightly. "I missed you guys. I've brought Daisy to stay with you for a couple of nights... and more importantly, this is Sam."

"Mr. and Mrs. Tennyson." I shake hands with both, but Ellie's mum Martha comes in for a hug, surprising me.

Her dad claps my back. "We heard a lot about you, young man. We're very proud of you."

I laugh awkwardly and throw an imploring glance at Ellie. *Help.*

She throws me a lifeline. "How about you go pick up the bags from the car, and I'll sort out some food and water for Daisy?"

Ellie's dad Mike accompanies me. On our way to the car and back, I make small talk. "Ellie didn't mention you had a winery. I'd love to try your wine."

It seems I said the right thing because his face lights up with a grin. "Ellie's such a rascal. We'll give you a short tour, then you can have a tasting with dinner." Mike grabs my bag and I carry Ellie's bag.

Daisy settles in for the night after having some biscuits. I walk to the verandah and take in the sweet summer evening smell. Cicadas are chirping wildly, and vines are the only silhouettes you can see for miles in the twilight.

I'm dying to spend some time alone with Ellie. I've barely seen her in the past two weeks. I don't even know if we are going to stay in different rooms tonight. Are her parents old fashioned? I have this image in my head of having to make ropes out of sheets and climbing through her window to get to her.

Ellie is putting some gifts wrapped in brown paper under the Christmas tree in the lounge, beaming with undisguised happiness at being home with her family. She tucks a strand of dark hair behind her ear, and my limited patience is now threadbare. "Ellie, do you want to show me around?"

Something in my tone makes her turn towards me, lips slightly open in surprise.

"Make it quick, dinner will be ready in five minutes." Martha's words bring me back to earth with a thud.

Five minutes is enough. Or is it? Ellie joins me on the verandah, and I check we're out of sight.

I wrap my arms around Ellie's waist and kiss her with urgency. I grab her by the ponytail and press my hardness against her, so she knows the effect she has on me.

I hear steps and we move apart, our breathing ragged.

She puts a hand on my chest. "Later."

The sound of footsteps goes away, but it's been too close. I must keep my hands and dick off her until later.

From the verandah, she points out the various outbuildings that are part of the working winery, and she tells me more about the history, and the variety, of wines they have here.

I hug her from behind and inhale the intoxicating scent of her. "Wow. It must have been a magical place to grow up."

"You're joking, right? I hated it. All my friends were in town. We moved here when I was fourteen. I couldn't drive, I was just stuck here, dependent on my parents taking me places." I can't make out the tone of her voice. Sometimes, like this moment, I really hate not being able to interpret other people's cues. I don't know when people are sarcastic. I can't tell in some situations if they're joking or not. More importantly, a lot of times, I can't tell when Ellie is happy or sad unless she explicitly tells me.

I kiss her head. "I suppose you're right, I hadn't thought of it that way. Your parents seem alright. And they love you very much."

"You'll catch a cold out there, you two. Time for dinner." Martha, Ellie's mum, echoes all mums in the world whose children are trying to steal more time together with their loved one.

Christmas Eve dinner is spectacular. Martha's food is Michelin star quality, and I say so. I'm not one for unnecessary compliments, and Ellie understands. The wines are delicious. I try a Malbec with the main and some bubbles Methode with the dessert.

We exchange some presents with Mike and Martha, but Ellie and I will open ours tomorrow, in O'Neill's Bay.

"They like you." Three single words from her on the way to our room, but they make me very happy.

"They're lovely people. I'm glad I met them and found this part of you. I'll buy some Ako wine off them, it would be good to take some to my mom and dad." I follow Ellie up the steps trailing behind her. She's just perfect. I don't know what I've done to get so lucky.

Her room is airy, full of photos with friends and family, Daisy, and some posters of boy bands. Some I recognize, some I don't. "At least there are no photos of ex boyfriends on the walls."

Ellie bursts out laughing. I guess I said that out loud.

My attention is drawn by the bed. It's too small for two people. I try to make light of the situation.

"So, what's the deal here, do I sleep on top of you? Or on the sofa downstairs with Daisy?"

She wraps her arms around my neck and presses her body against mine. I can't think straight.

"I think it's my parents' way of saying we should sleep apart," she says, "There's a mattress on the floor to the other side."

I don't like it one bit. I want more of Ellie, not less.

"Yeah … nah. You sleep on top of me then. I'm heavier."

We undress and I slip into the bed. She piles in on top of me, and I relish the weight of her and hug her tight. Soon, her breathing slows. She's asleep, but I'm not following her to dreamland. I can't close my eyes, worrying about the day ahead, and visiting my parents, and what that means. Christmas Day just became a test for our relationship.

CHAPTER 11

ELLIE

I wake up with a pain in my shoulder after sleeping cramped next to Sam in my bed. Ouch. I try to massage the knot away, but it's of little use.

It's Christmas morning. And Sam's birthday. We have a big day today. We'll drive back to Auckland to swap cars, and then be on our way. It'll take three hours to get to O'Neill's Bay. We'll be there by lunchtime.

Sam's still asleep, and it's quite rare to see him in such a moment of vulnerability. His face looks peaceful, serene. No furrowed brow or bitter set lips. He looks good enough to eat. I can't help myself, and I kiss him softly. He automatically responds to my kiss and pulls me in.

I kiss his nose. "Merry Christmas and Happy Birthday, my love. This one's going to be super special."

His tender, calloused hands stroke my face. "Merry Christmas. And thank you. You make it special."

"We have a long drive ahead of us today. Time to get moving." I get up and head for the shower to the tune of Sam's protests.

We get ready in a whirlwind, managing to sneak in some more hungry kisses, and by the time we're downstairs, my folks are already pacing.

"Did you have a good sleep?" My mum asks. I fervently hope there isn't a double meaning there.

Sam smiles. "Oh yes. Lovely house you have. Very quiet."

I try to cut the niceties short. "Mum, we'll have breakfast and then be on our way. We need to be in O'Neill's Bay by lunchtime."

We have some leftover Christmas ham sandwiches for breakfast, a strong coffee, and then we're walking towards the car.

My sweet Daisy wags her tail next to dad. I bend down and pat her head. "I'll come back soon for you, Daisy. Behave for Nana and Grandpa, alright? I'll bring you treats when I fetch you." Her eyes seem to light up at the word *treats*, and she gives a short bark. I pat her head one more time, then we're off.

And the issue of Dorothy the car roars back to life. As soon as Sam sits down, he's full of smartass comments. "Do you think we'll make it to Bella Vista at all? Will we need a rescue helicopter for Christmas Day? I wonder if this car would get towed in Bella Vista?" He's enjoying himself immensely, I can tell.

"Don't listen to him, Dorothy." I pat the dash. "You've been a trusted companion. You'll retire to a good home."

By hook or by crook, we get to his house in Bella Vista in an hour. I leave Dorothy the Ford Laser parked outside his house, and we change to his car after we load up more presents and stuff. Sam is visibly more relaxed in his car. It's less likely to break down. In the New Year, I'll look at getting a new-ish car. Maybe a small Toyota Corolla. *With my own money.*

"Tell me more about your family. What do they do? Anything I should be wary of?" I ask jokingly.

Sam tenses instantly. I hit a nerve. I put my hand on his knee, and he seems to relax somewhat.

"My mum Joan is a nurse," he says. "Loves kids. My dad Steve is a builder." He smiles fondly. "An unlikely match, you could say, but they work well together."

"My older brother Tom is the local bank branch manager. He's married to Sophie, a Korean doctor who works at the same hospital as mum. She's lovely. My brother is ... well. My brother." He shrugs, but I can sense love there. I wonder why he's so reluctant to go back.

"Must be a huge thing for them that you're a bit of a celebrity."

His sad smile breaks my heart. I'm coming around to the thought that his family must not be supportive, which is shocking for me. If I told my folks that I wanted to be a trapeze artist tomorrow, they'd support me unconditionally.

"They'd prefer I wasn't. I don't want to burden you with all this stuff. It's Christmas. You won't believe this, but I messaged Tayla to ask her what you want as a present." Sam smoothly changes topic.

"Oh yeah? And what did you get me in the end?" I can't imagine what Tayla said, whether she genuinely said something I might like, or if she pulled a prank on me.

He winks. "You'll have to wait and see. Not long left."

The landscape changes around us and beautiful wildflowers line the roadside. Going down from volcanic formations through hills and gorges, we inch closer to the sea again. When the first sign for O'Neill's Bay comes up, I start feeling nervous. What will his family think?

Sam takes the turn for the town center, and drives slowly, giving me a quick tour of all the local landmarks.

"That's the fish and chip shop. They do the best Kumara

111

chips, nice and crunchy. That's the bank where my brother works. The other side of the lake is the hospital my mum and Sophie, my sister in law, work at. And that one right there is the sailing club where I started out."

It feels like he's showing me his whole world, slowly putting together more pieces of his puzzle. A few minutes later he turns down a driveway. "This is us."

It's a large house, but not a mansion. Roses adorn one side of the fence. It's so close to the sea, I can smell the salty air. Four cars block the driveway, so Sam has to reverse and park on the street.

"Full house, I see."

He doesn't reply, he's so tense.

"It's okay, babe, whatever will be, will be. If it gets too much in there, we can go out for a walk. Just tell me."

He nods.

The moment we get out of the car, the door to the house opens, and Sam's family bursts out.

His mom wraps her arms around him. "Sammy Boy, come here." His dad and his brother take turns at squeezing him hard. It's obvious they don't get to see him that often. Sophie, his sister-in-law, gives him a brief hug and a kiss on the cheek.

Sam gently brings me forward. "This is Ellie, everyone. Ellie, these are my parents, my brother, and sister-in-law."

Joan, Sam's mum, hugs me tightly, and everyone else shakes my hand.

"Don't keep Ellie outside, Sam," Joan says. "Unload the car and come inside." She ushers us inside, while the men bring our bags and lug them upstairs.

The house is warm and welcoming, as are the people living in it. I take to his family straight away.

"Let's do presents now, we had to wait until you got here." Tom, Sam's older brother, pouts. They look alike in some ways, the same auburn hair and inquisitive eyes, but Tom looks more approachable, less aloof.

Sam brings down one bag from upstairs, and we hand out presents. I helped him choose the ones for his family—a spa voucher for his mum, golf vouchers for his dad, wake-boarding lessons for his brother, and a merino shawl for his sister-in-law.

I wait nervously as he opens his presents. He's very hard to buy for. What do you buy a man who can just buy what he needs without having to save up, like I do? His family joined forces and bought him an iPad Pro, which he seems to enjoy. He holds out the last two, looking surprised.

"One's a Christmas one, one's a birthday one." I try to hide the emotion in my voice.

He's taken aback and gives me a lopsided smile. "I don't celebrate birthdays, but this time I'll let you off the hook." Sam unwraps the first one, a small pendant with a wizened saint on it. He looks puzzled.

"That's St. Brendan," I explain, "the patron saint of sailors. He's going to protect you so that you come home safe every time." It feels like I've dropped a bomb in the room, and now we're dealing with the aftermath.

He looks downcast, his mum is discretely wiping a tear from her eye, and everyone else tries to pretend they haven't heard or seen anything.

Sam clasps the pendant around his neck and offers a weak smile. "That's very thoughtful. Thank you. Let's see what this one is." He shakes the small square package to check whether it makes a noise.

"I think it's a bicycle." I ease the tension, and everyone laughs.

Sam opens his present to find a book of ancient sailing maps about how cartography changed through time. He flicks through the pages, fascinated.

Steve, his dad, chimes in. "Seems you know my boy very well."

"Too well," adds Tom, and looks away naughtily.

"Oi, you. Don't scare her off," Sam barks.

I love to see the banter between Sam and Tom. "I'm not scared that easily." I raise one eyebrow at them.

I start to open my present from Sam. It's the size of a large shoe box. I shake it, and it rattles. I can't even begin to guess what Tayla told him to buy me. The box contains another box, to everyone's delight. I pretend huff and open that box, only to find a smaller box. Everyone's laughing out loud now, and Sam is looking at me with a challenge in his eyes, daring me to continue.

I open the small box, and inside is the most beautiful bracelet I've ever seen. A wave of apprehension hits me. "Are these stones real? I can't possibly accept this, Sam. It's too much."

"It's vintage." He silences my concerns in one go.

Joan stands and approaches, eyeing the bracelet. "Truly lovely," she says with a warm smile. She claps her hands together and turns toward the dining room. "Presents are over. Let's eat!"

Sam and I sit next to each other, and he squeezes my hand under the table.

Joan weaves her fingers together and closes her eyes. "We give thanks today for this meal, for family being together, for new additions to the family, and we think of the ones we love who are lost to us." After Joan's words, everyone holds a moment of silence, then we start eating. There's some traditional Kiwi Christmas fare, like Champagne Ham, but there are also some Korean dishes, like Bulgogi, prepared by Sophie.

Tom starts the grilling. "So Ellie, tell us more about yourself. How did you end up with Sam?"

I knew there would be plenty of that involved, like I knew they would compare me to Laura, Sam's ex-fiancée. An Olympian. I swallow the lump in my throat and hold my head high. "I'm a daycare teacher on the North Shore, born and bred in Auckland. My parents have a small winery, Ako Wines, up North by Matakana."

"We're having some of their wine now, actually," Sam helpfully points out.

"I love it." Steve's already on his second glass, and we all laugh.

"How did you guys meet?" Sophie, the sister-in-law, has been quiet until now, but she's engrossed in the story. Sam and I look at each other.

"How about you tell the story," I suggest, "and I'll pipe up if you're falling on the wayside?"

Everyone's attention focuses on Sam.

He smiles. "We met at some mutual friends' house. We liked each other … maybe a bit more. I didn't call." He picks up my hand.

Tom mock gasps. "You ratbag. My younger brother, the player, ladies and gentlemen." Everyone laughs, because it's obvious Sam is anything but a player.

He puts his arm around my shoulder. "But then I saw sense, and here we are." He pulls me closer and places a small kiss on my forehead.

Tom leans across the table, tapping his knife against his plate. "How about we go diving for some Kai Moana tomorrow, Sam? You, me, and dad on the boat, like the old times."

Sam looks at me, checking if Tom's plan is alright.

I nod. "You guys go, I'll stay behind with Joan and Sophie. Maybe have a look around. Looking forward to some yummy scallops and mussels tomorrow. I love seafood."

Sam seems relieved.

We finish the food, and help Joan with the tidy up, then I

see Sam getting fidgety. I move close to him and whisper. "I've eaten too much delicious food, I think. It's time to walk it off a bit."

Sam grabs my hand and starts walking so fast, I can barely keep up with him. Once we're past the corner, and his pace still hasn't let up, it dawns on me he's more wound up than I realized.

I pull on his arm, trying to slow him down. "Hey. Hey. I love you."

He stops in his tracks. "I'm sorry. I love you too. It was getting too much in there." He wraps his arms around me and kisses me in full view of the street.

"That's ok. We're a team, you and I. No man left behind." He laughs at my sailing joke.

"You and I should go out on a boat together at some point." He raises an eyebrow, knowing what I'm thinking. "No, the ferry to Waiheke Island for half an hour doesn't count. A sailboat." He pulls me closer as we walk together around the block and back towards his parents' house.

"You can see the wind on the ocean, did you know that?" Sam's voice seems to come from far away.

"I had no idea. Is it in the waves or how the boat moves?" I sense this is one of his sailing secrets.

"I can't explain it, but some of us see it, and some of us don't." His gray eyes look at me intently.

"It's good you can see it. It means you can go faster than those who don't." I wink at him, and he seems pleased. "If you'd lived 400 years ago, you'd be Captain Samuel Northcroft, going round the world exploring for five years at a time, and I'd be left at home, weaving and raising the children."

He looks towards the rose bushes. "Five years away from you. You know, some sailors are still gone for long stretches of time. You'd be surprised. I've never done it, but … I did enter a Round the World race. Would be gone for a year. It's not five years, but ..." He shakes his head. "Haven't been selected yet."

What?

I must have said it in my head, because he's still looking away. Damn right I'm surprised. And delighted it didn't come to pass.

Sam turns towards me again, picking up my hand and squeezing it. "Just like that, in a few minutes, you took away all the anxiety of being home. What am I going to do without you?"

That's a strange thing to say, and I don't grasp the meaning. I file it away for later and lead him towards the door of his childhood home. "You don't need to do anything. I'm not going anywhere." I kiss him quickly before we enter, and he pulls me closer, deepening the kiss.

He pulls away from the kiss too soon and we enter the house. Tom calls us into the living room. "You're in time for a treat, some board games, followed by *Die Hard* on TV." Tom knows how to keep the party going.

We play board games for a couple of hours, have some leftovers from lunch for dinner, then we settle on the sofas to watch *Die Hard*. Sam pulls me closer in an embrace, and I rest my head on his shoulder for a while.

Half-an-hour into the movie, Tom and Sophie excuse themselves. "We've got a big day tomorrow on the boat, need to get my energy levels up." Tom teases.

Sam rolls his eyes.

Joan waves them goodbye. "We don't mind, love. See you tomorrow."

"In that case, we're going as well. See you tomorrow, mum. Dad." Sam makes a beeline to escape, holding my hand.

"These young'uns, eh, Joan?"

On the way out I see Steve and Joan hug. They seem like a

lovely couple, and they love their children very much. Will Sam and I grow old together and host Christmas at our house one day? Or will our time together be short? Sam asked what he'd do without me? I hope he never has to find out.

CHAPTER 12

SAM

*I*t feels strange being back home with Ellie. This is the house where I grew up. This is the house where I came back every day after sailing practice. This is the house where I came back without Thea that day.

Ellie moves around, chatting to everyone like she belongs. That's one of the things that fascinates me about her. In any situation, with anyone, she'd find something to talk about, a way to connect to the person she's talking with. When I'm nervous I just drone on, and labor a point to death. Ellie puts everyone at ease. In some ways, her and Corey are alike, gliding through life like a catamaran through smooth waters. Me, I'm more of a dinghy fighting against the strong open ocean currents.

Earlier, as I saw Ellie with my family, charming each and every one of them, no matter how much of a dick my brother was, I wondered whether she would stick around after she finds out about Thea. Nobody has mentioned anything so far, but it's hanging over us like an invisible spider web we can't quite dust away.

When Tom bailed early during *Die Hard*, I knew I had to

seize the opportunity to have Ellie to myself just for a little while, so I excused us even though it wasn't even 8:00 p.m. As we walk towards my room, I feel apprehensive. How will she feel about it? I think back to her room and start laughing.

She shoots me an odd look.

"Just thinking back to your room and that single bed. My shoulder still aches from being squeezed in. Plus ... I'm a bit nervous about what you'll think about my room." We stop in front of a closed door. "Ready?"

She smiles, as I open the door. I haven't been here for such a long time, but somehow it all looks the same. Ellie is instantly drawn to the prize wall. A panel full of medals, cups, prizes and diplomas covers half of the wall, the biggest feature in the room.

"Wow. Are these all yours? I mean, of course they're yours. They're in your room." She covers her mouth. I can't tell if she's pleased or surprised or upset.

"Is it a bit much? I could always move it somewhere, a cupboard, or under the house." I don't mention that it's only a part of them. There are more floating around in various places.

"No way. These are your achievements. I'm very proud and happy for you. I just didn't think there would be so many." She smiles broadly.

I relax. "The other impressive feature in my room is a double bed. I got one when I turned fifteen because I needed to sleep comfortably. Unlike you."

She pokes her tongue out. I take it she likes it when I tease her.

She walks towards the window. You can see for miles out to the ocean, past houses, past the harbor, towards the mountains on one side. She sits on the window seat, and looks out, fascinated. "I love this view. It's amazing, I bet it changes all the time."

"I love it, too." But I'm not looking at the view.

She realizes I'm looking at her and laughs. "Smooth, Sam, smooth. You're learning."

I sit down next to her in the small window seat and pull her onto my lap.

She taps my chin. "Did you like your birthday and Christmas presents?"

I'm a bit caught out. I stroke her hair. "They're very thoughtful. No doubt about it, I'm going to pour over the ancient maps and dream about being there, sailing. And the protective necklace ..." I kiss her forehead. "We sailors are a superstitious bunch. Can't hurt to wear it. Corey wears a pounamu. What about my present for you?"

She looks down. I hope she's not upset. Tayla suggested jewelry or some spa vouchers, but I thought a bracelet would be something she can wear all the time. Seems I was wrong.

"I love it, it's the most beautiful thing I've ever seen." She winks. "Apart from you."

I look down. "I don't think anyone could call me beautiful. I'm just ordinary. Corey is much better looking."

Ellie holds me tight. "Well, I think you're beautiful, and my opinion matters the most." She kisses the tip of my nose. "And I'll wear the bracelet, but not at work. I'm worried I'll lose it or break it at playing with the kids. Or even better, there would be a rain of diamonds in some poor child's diaper." That's one angle I hadn't thought about, and we both giggle like little kids.

Ellie kisses my chest then nestles in closer. "Feels good to spend your birthday and Christmas with you. By the way, why did you say you don't celebrate your birthday? I love birthdays. I'd have two like the Queen, if I could."

Of course, Ellie loves birthdays. The cake, the presents, all the people together to celebrate you getting one year older. I'm quite lucky that my birthday is on Christmas day because

I never have to throw parties, and people don't expect it either.

"I just don't feel like it. Getting older makes me feel bad." I decide to tell the truth. Or part of it. For now.

"Listen to yourself. You sound like you're on death's door. You're only thirty-two. What are you going to say when you're seventy?" She shrugs. "Up to you, I guess. But we're definitely celebrating my birthday in May. Hope you penciled it in your calendar."

"Wouldn't miss it for the world." Ellie means so much to me, I can't imagine not being there for her.

She leans in for a kiss, and I pull her closer on my lap. She wraps her legs around me, and I can feel myself getting hard for her. I don't think there will ever be a time when I don't want her, crave her, need her like I do now.

I lift her up, her legs still wrapped around my waist, and climb on the bed.

She puts a finger on my lips. "It's your birthday. You get the treats." She takes off her clothes but doesn't let me touch her. "Na-ah. Your turn." She takes off my t-shirt and shorts, freeing my dick, which is aching for her. She kisses my lips, my jaw, then makes her way slowly but torturously downwards. She kisses my chest, sucks on my nipples, and by then I'm ready to explode. I try to hold her, but she moves away, giggling. She's going to be the death of me.

By the time she reaches my navel and grabs my dick, I'm starting to have a fair idea of what she wants to do, even through my desire induced brain fog. She takes all of me in her mouth, and I gasp. She starts stroking and sucking, driving me insane.

"Darling, I..." I'm unable to finish the sentence. No room for thoughts. Only ... how can I make her come?

I summon all my strength to not come too quickly and pull her up. She looks at me, puzzled and a bit disappointed.

"I want to taste you as you're tasting me."

A slow smile lights up Ellie's face, and she lies on top of me, facing away. I pull her closer to my face and taste her pussy. She's wet for me, and I need more. She is teasing my dick again and moaning every time my tongue flicks over her clit. She tastes amazing, and I want to make her come before I do. She seems to have the same thought. She works my dick faster, and more forcefully, licking the tip and sending me spiraling into oblivion. She comes seconds before I do, and I lap up all her juices before coming hard into her mouth.

I pull her up in my arms and we lay spent for what feels like a long time.

"Happy Birthday," she says after a while.

We laugh like it's the funniest thing in the world. We're carefree and in love. Except I'm carrying the heaviest burden of all. Once Ellie finds out ...

ELLIE

*I*t's Boxing Day today, and Tom convinced Sam and Steve, their dad, to go out on their boat diving for seafood bright and early. I'll spend most of the day with Joan, Sam's mum, then go out for a quick shop for Boxing Day sales with Sophie, Tom's wife, before the men come back.

After a cursory breakfast, I want to accompany them to the beach so I can wave them off.

"Time to get going. Sam said you want to wave us off, Ellie, so better get a move on". Steve, Sam's dad, rushes me along, playfully.

Sam and Tom bring out some wetsuits and diving gear, check everything is in order, then start walking towards the beach. Steve goes around the house, and comes back driving a tractor.

"Hop on, Ellie." I laugh, climb on, and off we go on the streets of O'Neill's Bay, on a massive red old tractor. Tom and Sam have already changed in their wetsuits, and I hop off, while Steve is bringing the boat around.

I kiss Sam firmly on his lips. "Take care out there. I want you to come back."

He smiles and strokes my cheek. "Will bring you scallops."

Using the tractor, Steve launches the boat, the boys hop on, and he parks the tractor close by. The boys help him climb aboard, and they sail off as I wave. The boat motors off into the distance, a trail of spray in its wake. I watch until I can't see it any longer, and my chest tightens. I'm afraid I won't be able to relax until he's back safely. I take a deep sigh, and walk back to Sam's parents' house to hang out with Joan, and Sophie later on.

I find Joan in the kitchen, making coffee. "Would you like some, dear?"

"I would love some, thank you." It's my first coffee of the day, and I can sense it's going to be one of many, since Sam is away and I'm so worried.

"You really worry about him, don't you, Ellie?" Joan seems fond of me already.

"I do. The ocean feels scary to me, so many depths, and so much … nothingness." I choose my words carefully. After all, that's how Joan's son, my Sam, makes a living.

Joan nods sadly. "Many lives lost at sea." She hands me a steaming mug of fresh coffee and a Tim-Tam biscuit.

"On the other hand, it calms Sam down a lot. I've read some studies that water can be very soothing for someone who's neurodivergent."

Joan drops her coffee mug into the sink. I jump up to help. "Are you alright? What happened?"

She looks sad, defeated almost, wiping the sink absently. "When did you find out about him? Did he tell you about it? He's never told anyone as far as I can tell."

They don't tell people about it! Are they ashamed? I would never have thought … they seem so proud of their son. "I thought it was common knowledge. His behavior patterns. He can't read cues very well. He talks in circles about a given topic. I'm a preschool teacher, and I have taught several children on the spectrum. They're all treasures, the lot of them."

"You won't tell anyone, will you?" She looks at me imploringly.

"Joan, being neurodivergent is nothing to be ashamed of. He's an accomplished man, he's achieved so much in life and he's only thirty-two. Plus, I love him to bits. I would *never* do anything to harm him in any way."

She seems more at ease and changes the topic. "Thank you. Sophie will come by soon. She's dying to show you the finest of what O'Neill's Bay has to offer."

We both laugh at that. I'm glad Joan has a good sense of humor.

"I really like you, Ellie," she says, "I hope my son finally decides to settle." She smiles at me, and the doorbell rings.

Joan goes to answer, and I admire the photos on the wall in the lounge. A couple strike me in particular. They feature what looks like Tom, Sam, and another child, could be a little girl. They definitely look related, freckles and auburn hair glistening from water drops. I puzzle over this. Could it be a cousin they're close to? I wonder why Sam never mentioned her before.

Before I could form another coherent thought, Joan enters the room with Sophie, looking fantastic in the morning sun.

Sophie takes my arm and starts strolling confidently towards the door. "Hey babe, I've been home to drop off the presents, but now I'm ready to go shopping."

I gather my handbag, wave goodbye to Joan, and get ready for some fun at the markets. We go on foot through

O'Neill's Bay, towards the town center. We walk on narrow streets lined with Pohutukawa in bloom, and Sophie stops to say "Hi" here and there. Some people throw curious looks my way. They must wonder who I am.

In some ways I miss living somewhere small like this, where everyone knows everyone. In other ways, I don't, because everyone's up in everyone else's business.

Sophie and I chat about everything under the sun, about my job at the daycare, my parents' winery, her job at the hospital, and she even confesses she and Tom are trying for a baby.

"Go you," I say, "very happy for you guys. Fingers crossed it happens soon. At least in the meantime you can have fun trying." I wink.

Sophie bursts out laughing at my tongue in cheek comment.

"What about you and Sam? Do you think you'll do the marriage, baby thing?"

Her question throws me off. In my heart of hearts, I do imagine Sam getting down on one knee at some point. Does he want kids though? He hasn't said anything about it, and I feel this is something we should be on the same page about. He hasn't even told me he loves me yet.

"We've only been seeing each other for a few months now, so it's yet to be seen." I keep my tone nice and light.

"Oh, come on, you must know by now he never brought girls home. Laura was more like a friend than a fiancée." Sophie enters the first shop, a local deli. "Let's get some snacks for lunch, to have while the boys prepare the seafood."

As Sophie shops, I offer to pay for half and choose some treats to take back home to Tayla.

"Tell me more about Laura." My jealousy is getting the better of me. From the photos I saw a while ago, she's a tall, leggy blonde. Very sporty and very suited to Sam.

Sophie brushes my concerns away. "Nothing for you to be worried about. I don't think she was a bad person, but she was a bit pushy, a bit too ambitious. Not good for our Sam, who needs to learn to take it easy."

Interesting. Sounds like a very driven woman. I admire that, but I'm more of a soft touch, due to the nature of my job, I guess.

Sophie and I taste some cherries and Manuka honey. "Sold. Delicious, let's buy some."

We go onto the next shop, already laden with bags. This time it's a Wellness shop, lots of beauty, skincare, crystals, and yoga mats. I sigh and buy a rose quartz for Tayla and, impulsively, grab a box of kawakawa balm for Corey. We may not be great friends, but as a sailor he can definitely use it on his hands.

As we make our way back towards the house, I remember the photos on the lounge wall. "A bit of an odd question. Who's that little girl in those childhood photos by the beach of Sam and Tom? She looks a lot like them."

I'm walking for a short while, before I realize Sophie has stopped on the street, mouth agape.

A feeling of dread pools in my stomach. "Did I say something wrong?"

"You don't know? Sam hasn't told you?"

Her words send me further into panic. "No. Is there anything I should know?" My voice is faint.

"I ... don't think it's my story to tell. Let's go back home."

As we walk together in silence, carrying heavy shopping bags, my heart beats faster. When we get to the door, everything is crystal clear.

"Sophie, listen. You don't have to tell me. I'm going to ask you something, and if I'm right, just nod."

She looks miserable.

"Is it their sister?"

Sophie nods.

My gut twists. "Did she ... pass away?"

A nod again.

"Is it anything to do with ... the water? " Sophie nods again, slowly, then opens the front door, leaving me torn in half.

CHAPTER 13

SAM

The first thing I can hear underwater is my own breathing, my own air bubbles. If they were to stop, it would be quiet in the ocean. That blue Moki over there would continue hiding among the kelp. The school of silvery yellowtails disperse in all directions as soon as I swim towards them, and regroup further along, away from the perceived danger.

Tom and I are diving while Dad waits for us on the boat. I haven't dived for a long time, maybe a year or more. Corey and I usually go spearfishing, but this time I promised Ellie some fresh scallops, so seafood it is.

We gather a legal amount of mussels, scallops, oysters, and clams. Tom is the first to surface and get back on the boat. I'd love to stay more, but I want to see Ellie again soon, so I follow suit.

Dad goes through our shellfish, making sure there are no undersized ones to throw back into the sea. "Good catch, boys. Just like the old days."

"I wonder what the ladies are doing," I say.

Tom finds my observation hysterical. "Bro, you're such a

goner. We've only been away three hours. It's not even midday. I'm sure Ellie can spare you for a couple of hours."

"Ah, but can I spare *her*?" I wink at him, and all three of us share a good laugh.

Dad sets course for the harbor. "Fine, boys, I think we have enough now. I'm turning back."

Tom and I cheekily shuck a couple of fresh oysters to tide us over until lunch time. Dad was right, it does feel like the old days. Spending time together as a family, carefree. Like before Thea passed away. I try not to think too much about her. I know I need to have the conversation with Ellie, but I had hoped to avoid it for as long as possible.

In about half an hour's time, we get back to shore and help Dad hook the boat to the tractor, to tow it back into the shed, and hose it down. Tom and I take our wetsuits off, keep our board shorts on, and shower quickly at the beach facilities. We walk home together, carrying the Kai Moana like a family treasure.

Ellie is in the kitchen, but she won't look me in the eye. What's going on? What happened? One name sounds like a mourning bell in my mind. Thea. Ellie must have heard about Thea.

I pry her away so I can talk to her. "Ellie, how about we go pick some veggies from the garden?" My heart rate has gone right up, and I can feel a humming in my head.

We walk out towards the veggie patch, and Ellie starts picking out some lettuce, tomatoes, oregano, and dill, and places them in my basket. Silence is unlike her.

I face it square on. She'll appreciate the truth. "What do you want to know?"

She turns her brown gaze towards me. "Everything."

I run my hand through my hair, and she watches me intently.

"I was five. Thea was seven. Tom was nine. He didn't want to come play with us that day, so Thea and I went by ourselves to the beach ... Without mum and dad knowing." My voice breaks. I struggle to hold on to the emotions, and I'm transported back to that day over twenty-five years ago. "Thea was always the better swimmer ... but that day ... there was a rip." I think comprehension sets in behind her eyes, as we remember the day at the beach when Ellie was caught in a rip.

"I ... couldn't help. I shouted for help. I ran back home to mum and dad. By the time we returned ... Thea was gone. She was never found."

Ellie puts her arms around me and hugs me hard. "I love you."

Her words calm me down, like a kawakawa balm on fresh wounds. "I love you too."

She smiles through tears. "I'm always here for you if you want to talk about it. We're a team, remember?"

I kiss her hard. It's like I've turned a corner. Ellie knows about Thea, and it's not a dealbreaker. Maybe it's not my fault. Maybe I was five, only a little bit older than Ellie's preschoolers.

We walk back inside and start preparing lunch. It dawns on me that tomorrow Ellie goes back to her house, I go back to mine, and any time together will be confined to short spans. This fills me with dread.

The afternoon passes comfortably into the evening, and once again I'm impressed and proud at how well Ellie gets on with my family.

Sophie is fully out of her shell, and Tom told me they're trying for a baby. For a fleeting moment I wonder what Ellie would look like pregnant. Does she want children? She looks after children for a job, so maybe she doesn't want any of her own. Or maybe she *does* want some.

Tom sidles up next to me and elbows my ribs. "Time for Cards Against Humanity, I think."

I'm jolted into the present and elbow him right back. "No fucking way, bro. We're not playing that with our *parents*." I nod towards them.

"Of course not. They're going on a date. It's just the four of us." Tom winks.

"A date? Whatever next." My rolled eyes reveal my sarcasm.

Mum laughs. "It's just fish and chips on the beach, love."

Mum and Dad pack a picnic basket and leave for the fish and chip shop at sunset.

Ellie is impressed. "Goals, right there."

I'm impressed as well. They're in their 60s and still go on dates. Just being with one person forever seems huge. Making time, being *present* for them.

We spend a fun couple of hours playing Cards Against Humanity with Tom and Sophie.

I decide on the spot we should see them more often. "Guys, I know you lead busy lives but don't be strangers. You're welcome to come up to Auckland for a long weekend and crash at mine. See some sights. Eat some food. Do touristy stuff."

My brother looks very pleased. It's the first time I've ever invited him to come stay with me in Auckland.

Sophie takes another sip of her wine and grins. "Definitely, my brother lives there as well. Plus some more shopping to be done in the big smoke. Right, Ellie?" Sophie and Ellie are thick as thieves.

It's been a long time since I've felt so relaxed. It's so far away from my usual training all hours of the day, jetting around the world. It's ... appealing. It's scary.

ELLIE

*W*e spend the final night of the trip mostly awake, savoring all remaining moments together. We make plans on what to do together next, how we'll spend New Year's, and beyond that.

Why does it always feel like he's saying goodbye, every single time? Is it the nature of his work? Or is it because of what happened to Thea? More importantly, is it something I can live with, this uncertainty of him coming back?

The morning light finds us embraced, unwilling to let go. After breakfast, Tom and Steve help Sam load up the car.

I say my farewells to Joan and Sophie. "It's been a pleasure, and I hope to see you again very soon. Maybe you can come up to Auckland." They seem pleased with my invitation and take turns to hug me.

"See you later, bro. Take care." Tom hugs Sam and pats him on the back. Joan and Steve embrace Sam wordlessly, with tears in their eyes.

On the road, Sam is quieter than usual. His lips set, his eyes covered by sunglasses, he looks like he's in one of his sailing races, fight or flight mode activated.

I put a hand on his leg. "Everything alright? Do you want me to take over, while you rest a bit?"

He glances at me briefly. "All good. Just thinking."

Oh boy. I can tell this is going to be one of those conversations where I talk my head off, and he'll barely say anything.

I pull my hand off his leg and look out the window. "From tomorrow until New Year's Eve, I have to go to work. The kids will be very excited, they'll tell me all about Christmas."

Sam nods.

"What do you have on this week?" I work hard to coax him out of silence.

He sighs. "Some meetings. Some press calls. Then more meetings. Maybe I can squeeze in a training day with Corey before next year." He runs his fingers through his hair impatiently. "When do I see you next? New Year's Eve?"

I squeeze his thigh. "You can come by any evening, stay over. You know that. Tayla doesn't mind."

He takes off his sunglasses, and glances at me again. Something's really bugging him. "I was thinking ... you could come stay at mine. Look after the house when I'm away, that sort of stuff."

That's not the least romantic thing I've heard in my life, but it's definitely up there. The worst part of it is he probably can't even tell his suggest has ticked me off by looking at me. "Water the palms? Mow the lawn? Keep things clean? That sort of stuff?" My body is tense and my words short, clipped.

He lowers his shades and stares at me like I've grown another—no, two other—heads. "What's wrong?"

"You're such a dick, Sam. Suuuuch a dick. What you want is a housekeeper." I'm annoyed by this point. I have a vision of him gallivanting around while I'm chained to an old-fashioned stove. Left behind, just like when my parents upped-sticks and moved all of us to the middle of nowhere Matakana. I know I'm being unfair because he's not really asking me to be his maid. I don't care.

Sam looks flustered. It's probably not the reaction he was expecting, and he is retreating into his shell. "I'm sorry, I … it came out the wrong way." He's trying to choose his words carefully. "Corey would have said the right thing." His voice trails off.

Why even drag Corey into this. I'm getting unbearably hot in anger, and I put the window down. "Fuck Corey. This is about *us*." We're in his car, on a four hour journey, arguing. Just my luck. Out the window the landscape is passing by at speed, changing from jaunty volcanic hills, to corn fields, to tidy market gardens.

"I thought that … you could be there when I come home. All the time." Sam's soft words make me really look at him.

"… that I wouldn't have to miss you like crazy. Like I do." He picks up my hand. "That you could be an even bigger part of my life." Sam kisses my hand, sending shivers through me. Just like that, I stand no chance.

I turn into a puddle of goo. "What about Daisy? I can't leave her behind." My first thought is to my sweet girl who's been with me through thick and thin.

"Daisy can come as well. She's stayed overnight several times now. She's used to the place." Sam's feeling more confident now.

Another thought crosses my mind, and I sigh. "What about Tayla? I can't leave her alone. She needs me."

Sam, ever patient, finds solutions. "We'll help Tayla find another flatmate, to straighten out with the rent costs, and provide good company."

I lean back in my seat. "It's settled then. Maybe I can move in February?"

He lets out an exasperated laugh. "No fucking way. Tonight."

He's surely kidding. I can't possibly pack up everything I own and just leave with Daisy.

"It's not fair on Tayla. Plus, I need to pack all my stuff."

He rolls his gray eyes at me. "How long do you need?"

"Make it after New Year's, that long weekend. At least I won't need to go to work, and I can unpack, get Daisy settled."

He sighs, but deep down he knows I'm right.

We spend the time left to my parents' house chatting about the move, things to do in Bella Vista, how long the new commute to my work will be, and dog friendly cafés in the area. Deep within me lay lingering doubts, and a fear of being left behind. Again.

* * *

"WHAT DO you mean you're leaving? What a load of bollocks, Ellie. You've only been dating since September. What's next? Are you going to marry him in March?" Tayla has been outraged since I came back home. The presents I got her from O'Neill's Bay haven't managed to soothe her sensibilities in the slightest.

"Calm down, dear." My tongue in cheek comment fans the flames.

"No, *you* calm down." Tayla is pacing around the lounge like a pink-maned lioness. "You're moving too fast, Ellie. Search your heart. He's going to leave you behind alone in that fancy house in Bella Vista and traipse off as usual. Are you even into him, or are you just glad someone's sticking around?"

Tears color my cheeks.

Tayla notices, stops her pacing, and embraces me. "Oh,

Ellie, I'm sorry. I just care too much about you. I don't want you to get your heart broken." The unspoken words "like me" hang between us. Tayla has had her fair share of douche canoes. That doesn't mean Sam is one of them.

"Tayla, I know you mean well, but please be happy for me. I found someone I love and who loves me back."

She hugs me harder. "I am happy for you. Maybe a little jealous. I wish I met someone like that." Tayla winks at me, and we both laugh.

"We need to put a notice down the grapevine we're looking for a flatmate for you. I'm sure there will be someone we know who's super nice and keen. And I'll also pay my share of six weeks' rent to cover any shortfall."

It's the end of an era, moving away from Tayla, from the house I'd called home for the last six years. This is where we'd watched endless K-Dramas, cried after we had our hearts broken for real, and found out that we got our first jobs after university. This also holds memories of meeting Sam, and I'm looking forward to a new beginning. With him.

CHAPTER 14

ELLIE

*I*n the few days up to New Year's Eve, Sam and I haven't been able to see each other. I worked every day. He was busy with meetings and TV and radio interviews.

By the time the thirty-first came around, I'd been chomping at the bit. I can't wait to move in with Sam and see him nearly every day.

We're spending New Year's at Paddy and Gracie's, and it feels like the perfect way to end the year that brought me Sam. Who knows what next year has in store. Tayla and I will catch a taxi there. Corey is also invited, though we're not sure he'll turn up. I still need to give him the presents I bought for him in O'Neill's Bay.

Tayla and I have really pushed the boat out with our outfits, even though we're among friends. I want to impress Sam because I haven't seen him for a few days. I'm wearing the shortest dress I've got. I wonder who Tayla's trying to impress with her sheer dress.

When we get to Paddy and Gracie's, I have a deja vu. Last time I was there, I met the love of my life. This time, Sam's already there waiting. He sweeps me off my feet, literally, kissing me until I'm dizzy.

Corey pokes his head around the corner. "Hey, get a room, you two. Come in, Tayla, let these losers at it." Tayla moves past us into the house, laughing, and more importantly, leaving us alone.

Sam kisses me again. "I missed you, sweet. Only two more days until you move in. God, I can't wait."

"You'll be beside yourself when you see my three hundred skincare products in the bathroom, and no longer have a corner to put your stuff on."

He laughs. "I can't wait. Let's go in. Everyone's here already."

We pick up drinks on the way outside, and spend the next couple of hours chatting, cracking jokes, and dancing. I give Corey his presents, and he seems pleasantly surprised but jokes that he may forget them somewhere along the way.

Tayla and Corey seem to be spending an awfully long time together. His hand is on her shoulder, and he's whispering something in her ear, making her laugh.

"Look at that." I point them out to Sam.

"At what?" He's oblivious.

"Corey and Tayla have the hots for each other."

Sam rolls his eyes. "Corey's not into relationships. Don't get your hopes up."

I put my arms around his neck. "Neither were you. Into relationships. Now look at us." He kisses me.

Paddy hands out champagne glasses to everyone, starting with Gracie. "Get your champagne, everyone. We're starting the countdown."

Fireworks explode from the Sky Tower, and Sam and I kiss like there's no tomorrow, oblivious to everyone and everything around us.

* * *

SAM

*W*hen Ellie said she'd cover all surfaces in the bathroom with creams and *potions*, I thought she was joking. As I pack my bag for a few nights away training, I shake my head at the amount of *stuff*.

The move went smoothly. Corinne, a friend of a friend of Tayla's, took Ellie's room, and we hired a van to get everything here. Some more artwork appeared on the walls, dog toys scattered around the floor, and many, *many* clothes, shoes, and handbags hung in the closet.

Even though my life has been turned upside down, Ellie has been with me every night. I couldn't be happier.

"I'm off now. The guys are picking me up in a few minutes." I grab my duffel bag and kiss her squarely on the lips. Daisy dog whines and wags her tail. I give her some rubs and go out to the team van.

I'll be away for five nights this time, probably the longest I've been away from Ellie since we met. As I get into the van, I take one last look at my love standing in the doorway, all petite, her dark hair tousled, and I wish I could go back. I wish I could *stay*. How many more goodbyes will we have to say?

Jake notices my silence. Out of all of the team, he knows best what it's like to leave a loved one over and over again. "I would like to tell you it gets easier, mate. But it doesn't. It is what it is." He pats me on the back. "At least you guys are living together now. When you come back, you see her straight away."

The silver lining.

We drive three hours North towards one of our training facilities. It's going to be a grueling few days. We haven't trained in a month, and it will show. To take my mind off being away from Ellie, I devise tactics for maneuvering the boat at high speeds.

* * *

THE JOURNEY PASSES QUICKLY, and I sleep soundly that night, dreaming of Ellie.

The next day, our boat and the British boat are out on the water. I wave at Luke Bailie, the British team skipper, from a distance. He nods and waves back.

We're relentless, sailing for hours, testing the boat's limits until we can't push anymore. At the end of each day, after communal dinner, we crash in our bunks and drift off into dreamless sleep.

On day four, the weather makes it impossible for us to train. Gales and summer storms batter the area, and we stay indoors mostly, discussing tactics and technical plans.

Coach enters the room and claps his hands. "Boys, the weather's packing in for the week. We'll go back early tomorrow morning. No point hanging around here. I know some of you are pining." Coach winks at me. I roll my eyes. I thought I'd put this to rest.

At the same time, my phone, Corey's phone, and Florian's phone vibrate. We reach for our phones in our back pockets, puzzled.

Corey reads out loud. "Congratulations! You have been selected to participate in the Round the World Ocean Race, departing from Malaga, Spain on March 1st."

I've got the same message blinking up at me, but I'm struggling to process it.

Corey and Florian jump up, whooping and making a victory dance. "Yeah boi! We've done it!" The other team-mates and Coach cheer them on.

"You coming, Sam?" Florian doesn't let up.

I smile sadly. "Of course. How could I not? It's a once in a lifetime opportunity." I'd signed up for this a while ago, just before I met Ellie. It's an amazing opportunity for any sailor, so why do I feel like I've been split in half?

Corey knows something's up. He looks at me pointedly. "This isn't about Ellie, is it?"

I look straight at him, not saying a word.

Corey laughs. "There are stopovers after each leg every three to four weeks. She can come to Brazil, Hong Kong etc. Like an exotic holiday every month for a year. I'd be up for that."

I push away from the table to release some of my pent-up frustration. "When you put it like that... maybe I've got a chance. I'm doing it anyway." I'm being quite belligerent now. "I've wanted to do this since I was a kid. How many people can say they've sailed around Cape Horn?" My rhetorical question touches many of the team.

"Well, if you change your mind, I want to go in your place," Matt chimes in.

Florian looks at him strangely. "No fucking way. It's Sam's place. He earned it, just like Corey and I earned ours."

Things are turning sour so I put my hands up. "Guys, I'm

going, alright. Ellie's just going to have to deal with it, and so will I. We're grown-ups. Sailing is what I do, and tough luck."

My words seem to calm their spirits, and they continue chatting about what life at sea will be like. Conversation soon turns to belting out old bawdy sea shanties, to Coach's great delight.

I don't join in the singing, and I can't help but fervently wish this damn kombucha type health drink would turn into some strong whisky. Not allowed to drink while in training. But today I definitely need a double.

Where's that St. Brendan pendant? Here it is. I'd left it behind in my wallet today, and now I'm holding it, thinking how Ellie will react to me going away for a whole year. There will be some breaks, though, chances to see one another. What Corey said makes sense. She could come to the ports we dock at, and we could have a couple of days together here and there. A year of great vacations. It's not like I'm leaving her behind. Not really.

CHAPTER 15

ELLIE

*I*t feels a bit strange to think of Sam's house as my own. Daisy has settled in well, and I've met a few of the neighbors already. Naveen and Carl from next door offered to pet sit Daisy, and judging by how she acts around them, wagging her tail like crazy, I think I'll take them up on the offer.

Corinne, a friend of a friend, took my old room in Tayla's house, but I've basically been living with them the last few days while Sam's been away, as if I never moved.

Corinne has a wicked sense of humor and entertains us with tales from her various places of work: the opera where she performs as a soprano, photoshoots as a plus size lingerie model, and the small café where she moonlights as a barista.

Sam texted to let me know he's coming back early tomorrow due to the weather, so I have one more chance to spend time with the girls.

Corinne hold her arms out wide, wearing a blinding smile. "Ladies, how about we crash a party?" Corinne is always up for going out.

Tayla and I are homebodies.

"Nah, check out this weather." Tayla whines, gesturing at the drops hitting the window pane. "The last thing I want is to go out through the rain." The large Nikau tree in the middle of the roundabout of our small right of way sways dangerously.

I try to be polite. "What sort of party?"

"Something about ocean conservation. You'd be into that, Ellie." Corinne and Tayla laugh. "More like a fundraiser, I reckon, but we could always go for the drinks and nibbles."

I think of what I might have to wear. "You're so funny, girls. We need to muster up a donation, I think, but I'm keen to go."

Corinne shepherds us toward our rooms to get dressed, "Okay, it's settled. Tayla, move that fine ass of yours into gear."

In exactly two hours we're all made up and dressed to impress, packing into an Uber, on the way to the Sky Tower.

"I've only been once up here, on a date," Corinne confesses. She seems nervous.

"Must have been one hell of a date." Tayla straightens her figure-hugging dress.

The doorman takes down our names, and we are whisked up in one of the elevators fifty-three floors above Auckland City to a panoramic area. The wind and the rain swirl outside the massive windows.

Tayla insists on a selfie with all of us. "I haven't dolled up for nothing, ladies. Say cheeeeeeese." We take some seats, and I notice a couple of girls insistently looking at us. "What's up with those chicks right there? Do any of you know them?" Corinne voices my thoughts exactly.

"Nah, they don't look familiar to me. Maybe some models you've worked with or something?" I ask Corinne.

They make their way towards us, and there's no escape.

"Are you Sam Northcroft's girlfriend?" It feels like they're circling me like eagles. Tayla laughs, and says something inaudible to Corinne.

I aim to be friendly but brief. "Yes. What's up?"

"You look different on Instagram ... Smaller." The tall one frowns. "Does that mean he's very tall?"

I'm do a double take, and Tayla and Corinne laugh harder. "Erm, I suppose he is."

"Ok, ladies, you had your answers. Ellie's going to tell Sam she met you, alright? Have a good evening." Tayla shoos them away, rescuing me from one of the most embarrassing situations I've had recently, and I've had plenty.

The girls leave unsatisfied, chattering.

I shrug my shoulders. "That was ... weird. I don't get what they wanted. What's the point." I check my phone again. No message from Sam this evening, but I'll see him tomorrow.

"Probably wanting to see what he sees in you." Corinne sounds serious, and I turn towards her.

"I know I'm short. Don't have to keep reminding me." My laugh is a bit strained. "My mum's short. My dad's short. I can't help it. Don't have the lanky genes, like Sam's ex."

Tayla winks at me. "One word, two letters. E-X. There's a reason that she's an ex and you're not, so I wouldn't worry too much about her."

A mic buzzes in the background.

I stand on tiptoe and look toward the sound. "Is there a band here tonight?"

An announcer steps up, taps the mic. "We are proud to welcome Gold Olympic Rowing Medallist and all-round good New Zealander, Laura Killarney, here in Auckland, Tamaki Makaurau, the city of lovers. Tell us, Laura, how can we love our ocean a bit more? The host's announcement drops like a bomb in my ribcage.

Corinne and Tayla gasp, and the two girls who came earlier snicker.

Laura, a tall leggy blonde, strides confidently towards the stage, thanks the host, and cracks a few jokes to warm up the audience. I am mesmerized by how she works the room. Her tone becomes more serious as she starts talking about ocean conservation, and at the end of her speech, she urges everyone to donate as much as they can. She's animated, and I find myself quite liking her. I really don't understand how Sam could break up with someone like her, sporty and easygoing.

The host announces some raffle or another, but I stop listening.

"She was something." Tayla's words break through to me. "But don't compare yourself to her. Obviously Sam wants something different, and that's you." She points at me.

"Don't sweat it. Let's get a drink." Corinne is ever practical.

We walk up to the bar, I pick up one of the pear and ginger margarita cocktails on offer, and as I turn to comment on how amazing it looks, I land face to face with Laura. She's at least a head taller than me, and I'm wearing heels. I can't feel more intimidated.

"Hey. How's it going?" Laura asks with an easy smile. She seems open and friendly.

I throw caution to the wind. "Not too bad. What about you? I'm Ellie by the way."

Laura smiles. "I know who you are." She says it in a funny cloak and dagger voice, and I can't help but burst out laughing. I can see from the corner of my eye that Tayla and Corinne are letting out deep breaths they'd been holding in.

"Where is Sam tonight? Tell him I said hi." I find that a bit strange. Are they friends still?

"He's away training."

She turns to leave and mingle.

I stop her in her tracks and tap her on the shoulder. "Hey,

before you head off … quick question. Why did you guys break off the engagement?"

She looks at me with a mix of sadness and impatience. "You had to go there, huh." She crosses her arms and shakes her head, choosing her words carefully. "We shouldn't have been engaged in the first place. Sam … he's … different. He's away a lot. He's … unavailable. Emotionally. Anyway, *good luck*." She clearly means with Sam's emotional unavailability. "See you around." She leaves.

Her last words haunt me like the unfriendliest of ghosts. I walk back to Tayla and Corinne, and they can tell something's wrong.

"Do I need to follow the bitch into the bathroom and give her a piece of my mind? What did she say to you?" Tayla's always got my back.

"Nah, she was friendly. I was just dumb enough to ask why she and Sam broke up. Messed up." The girls hug me wordlessly, and as we leave and make our way back to Tayla and Corinne's through the rain, the feeling of inadequacy strangles me. I can't breathe, but it won't let go.

SAM

*I*t's absolutely pissing down with rain, and it's taking so much longer to get home. Traffic is crawling from Whangarei southbound. A journey that usually takes four hours has taken six and counting. We're not even in sight of the Harbor Bridge yet.

On one hand, I'm excited to go beyond the bridge, home into Bella Vista, and see Ellie when she comes home from work. On the other hand, I'm absolutely dreading telling her about the Round the World Ocean Race. I have no clue how she'll react.

We finally make our way over the bridge, and thankfully I'm one of the first drop-offs. I open the door to the house, and Daisy barks and wags her tail in excitement.

"Missed you too, girl. What have you been up to?" I give her pats and rubs, and she lies on her back, lapping up all the attention.

There are still a couple of hours left until Ellie comes back home from daycare, so I unpack, put a wash on, change clothes, and go out briefly for some groceries. I'm going to surprise her with a cooked dinner. My skills don't stretch very far, or as Corey says, I can cook enough not to starve, but I'm going to push the boat out tonight.

After looking up some recipes online, I choose something that seems fancy but easy enough to prepare—Salmon Wellington, fish in puff pastry. I buy ready-made pastry, of course, and set about making the dish, ready to pop into the oven when she's on the way home.

I go through my emails, studiously avoiding the Round the World Race details one. My brother just saying Hi. Some media requests. Some contracts. Nothing amazing. I flick the race email open and quickly scan the details. First of March start, but early departure advised. How early is early? Like two weeks early? Or like two days early? Surely there's some training involved. I ponder this for a while and don't hear the key turning in the lock.

"You're home." Ellie rushes towards me, and I'm engulfed once again in the nearness of her. My arms wrap around her automatically, like they always do, and a shiver passes through her while we kiss.

"Are you cold? Let's turn the heat pump on. It's unusually cold for January. This rain is just ridiculous. It hasn't stopped for two days." I want to look after her, I want her to be comfortable in our house.

"What's this?" She's looking at the salmon dish.

"Oh, shit. That should have been in the oven by now." I'm panicking. I was trying to impress her with some nice home cooked food, and it's slowly going to pot.

"That's okay. Let's put it in now, and we can have some cheese on crackers while it's cooking." In one sweep, Ellie makes everything better.

I can't take my hands off her. "I love you, do you know that?"

"Love you too. I'm impressed with the food. Looks yum."

She stands up on her tiptoes and kisses me. "Now tell me, how was training?"

I swallow a knot. Now would be a good time to tell her. I can feel Corey and Florian urging me from afar.

I stroke her hair while she nibbles on a cheese cracker. "It was good. We saw the Brits training as well and could glean a bit into their racing style ... but then it started raining heavily so we came back." I can't do it. I can't. "And how have you been?"

Ellie looks at me with her brilliant eyes and smiles. "I've been well. Last night we went to this ocean conservation charity event. You'd have liked it, probably. Or maybe not, cause you don't like going out." Her laughter makes my heart soar, even if it's at my expense.

"Oh? Tell me more." I kiss her forehead, her cheeks, her lips.

"I can't concentrate when you do this." Her eyes are half shut, and her lips slightly open, inviting me for more kisses.

I bite her lip gently. "What about this?"

"Hm ... Your ex Laura was there."

That's a mood killer if I ever heard one. "Did she say something to you?" Laura doesn't hold a grudge as far as I know.

Ellie looks at me for a second. I can't tell if she's happy, sad, or something in between.

The oven timer beeps, and I take out the salmon and let it cool on the rack.

Ellie pours two glasses of white wine, and hands me one.

"Cheers to you coming back in one piece." She takes a sip, watching me intently.

I need to muster up the courage. It's now or never. "Ah ... listen, I was going to talk to you about something." I run my fingers through my hair, like I always do when I'm nervous.

Ellie can read me like an open book, usually, but I don't think she imagines what I have to say this time.

She perches atop one of the breakfast bar stools and continues sipping her wine. "I'm all ears."

"Do you remember that race I told you about? The one I applied for a couple of months before I met you?"

Her brows furrow as she thinks, trying to remember. Her mouth parts and her gaze darts to mine. Yep. There it is. She remembers.

"Yesterday I found out I was selected for the team ..."

"The team for the Round the World Race?" Her face is a blank mask, and I can't read it.

"We sail around the world for up to a year. Every month we dock at a port around the globe for a couple of days ..."

Ellie looks like she's going to be sick. Her face is ashen, and her lip trembles. When she speaks, her voice is so small I can barely hear. "A year? *Why?*"

Daisy senses something's wrong, darts straight to Ellie's feet, and lies down.

"A year's not that long in the grand scheme of things ... You could ... come to the ports around the world each month. Brazil, Hong Kong, San Francisco ... we could have a couple of days together on land here and there." When Corey suggested this, I thought it was a great idea. Now, seeing Ellie's stricken face ... What have I done?

Ellie jumps off the counter, almost spilling her wine. She finishes it in one gulp and the glass clatters against the counter, toppling, when she slams it down. "How long have you known about this? Why haven't you told me this was a possibility from the beginning? And more importantly what the hell are you thinking, Sam? I can't just drop my job like an old hat to go around following you from port to port, while wondering if you're still alive." I've never seen Ellie this angry.

"I'm sorry, okay. It's something I've wanted to do since I was a child. You could always ... quit your job. You don't need to work. I earn enough for both of us." My toes squirm as I say it. This is going downhill very fast. What the hell am I doing?

Ellie's brown eyes are furious, and she's got her hands on her hips, telling me off like I'm one of her preschoolers. "You ... you wanker. Just like you, I love my job and don't want to leave it for the world. The fact that it pays less than yours doesn't mean it's less important. "

I pace away from her then back. "It's not like you didn't know this was a possibility. I told you I signed up for it."

"You did." She nods, her lips pressed thin. "But you also said it was unlikely you'd be picked. You made it sound like it wasn't a possibility."

I don't have an explanation. Seeing her so upset makes me even quieter. I withdraw as I do with any conflict, ever.

Now she's pacing around the room. "And what do you expect me to do, hang around this house for a year then you waltz back into my life fresh as a daisy? I'm telling you, no fucking way."

"Ellie, listen. I'm really sorry I haven't told you about it, I don't have an excuse. It's not a long time in the grand scheme of things, you can come to some if not all of the ports. I'll pay for your tickets. I'll be safe. Corey and Florian are also going. We'll look after each other." I hope to reason with her, I don't know what the alternative is.

A sob escapes her chest, and she runs towards our bedroom, Daisy and I hot on her heels. Under my shocked gaze, she picks out one of her suitcases from the wardrobe and stuffs her clothes into it.

I'm in a daze. Only a few hours ago I was on my way home, excited to see her again, making that stupid salmon pastry thing. Now she's leaving me.

I step forward, hoping to catch her scent, to catch her into my arms and never let her go. "Ellie... please."

She looks at me through tears, her voice shaking but determined. "It's not going to work, Sam. You think my job is worthless. You tell me that you're fucking off for a year. It's not working."

"Okay." I'm speechless. I don't know what to say to keep her from leaving this house, from leaving my life completely.

"Where are you going?" I worry about her. Tayla has a new flatmate. She can't just return there, can she?

"I'm going to crash at Tayla's in the spare room until I find something." Ellie finishes packing a suitcase. She takes Daisy and goes to her new car, a Toyota Corolla. She refuses any help from me. She looks at me briefly over her shoulder. "Tayla and Corinne will pick up the rest of my stuff."

I stand in the pouring rain, watching the love of my life drive away, and my heart breaks into crumbs.

I go back inside the house, now empty of Ellie, of Daisy, of everything I love. Instead, there's that stupid salmon pastry on the rack, cold by now, and our two half empty glasses of wine.

I can't believe what just happened. What if I never see her again? Have I ruined everything? But she can't expect me to just give up sailing. And this race ... I didn't apply for it to spite her. I did it before I even knew her. But damn, is the race worth losing her? I shut that thought down. I have to do the race. I have to because ... because ... My heart races. My palms sweat. The walls creep closer and closer, and I can't breathe. I need to get out, get some fresh air. So what it's raining, we're not made of sugar. That's what my old sailing coach used to say.

I put my cap on, grab the keys, wallet and phone, and step out again into the New Zealand rain. I am drenched in the first few seconds, making my heart beat faster. I run to forget about the dull ache in my chest. I don't know how I'm going to get over it. I run to the Marina and back through mostly empty streets. Running back up the hill gets my heart racing, but I still can't shake away the need for Ellie. Did she get to Tayla's safely? Should I text her?

I return home soaked and shivering. After a change and a shower, I pick up the Salmon Wellington by hand like it was a sausage roll and bite into it. Not bad.

I message Corey and Florian that I want to leave early, maybe this coming weekend, a full three weeks ahead of departure. They're excited and don't question it.

The longer I can delay telling everyone about Ellie and I, the better. It's going to be like an all-consuming hurricane, so I lay in wait for what's to come.

CHAPTER 16

"What. The. Hell." Tayla dropped a piece of toast, and Daisy rushed to grab it as I walk into the Hillcrest house with my suitcase.

Corinne's eyes are wide with surprise. She wraps her arms around me and sits me on the couch. "Babe, sit down. What happened? Did someone die?"

I smile bitterly. "Feels like someone died, yes."

Taya paces the space in front of the couch, arms flying like windmills. "Is he whoring? Has he been dipping where he shouldn't? I don't trust these quiet ones. Still water runs deep." Tayla is ready to jump at Sam's throat. She's so loyal, it brings tears to my eyes.

Corrine pats my shoulder. "Aw, don't cry babe, nobody deserves it. Do you think he's at home crying for you? I doubt it." Corinne's right, I doubt it too. He's probably happy to be rid of a nuisance.

"Nah, wasn't that. Hey, I didn't have dinner. With one thing and another. Could I please have a bit of what you're having?" My tummy rumbles audibly.

Tayla runs to the kitchen. "Sure, sweetie, have some baked

beans on toast, and some nice chamomile tea. Now tell us what happened." Tayla returns, handing me the food and drink.

"Sam came back from training. Wants to go sailing around the world for *a whole year* in a race. Wants me to wait at every port he's at, once a month for a couple of days." Even as I'm telling them about our argument out loud, I realize how terrible it sounds. I start eating the simple dinner, and the chamomile tea has a near instant calming effect.

"Hold up. He wants to WHAT? He just came home, like literally today. This afternoon." Corinne just can't compute. I know how it feels. I can't wrap my head around it, either.

I take a large bite of toast and wash it down with tea. "And he said I should quit my job." I'm still furious at the thought.

"No fucking way, Ellie. I'm telling you, no fucking way. He's playing you like a fiddle. How long has he known about this?" Tayla dots the i, as usual.

I shake my head. "He did tell me. But he made it sound like it wouldn't happen, so I … I put it out of my mind. Even though I knew about it, it still feels like a punch to the gut, unexpected and ugly. "Really, it's his suggestion that I quit my job that hurts the most. Like what I do doesn't matter." I choke on the last words and cry into my tea.

Tayla plops down on the couch beside me. "So he told you? Once. And then let you forget about. Ha. Like he was covering his tracks or something." She pops back up. "I'm gonna go slash his tires."

I pull her back down with a tear-filled laugh. Somehow she makes me feel a bit better.

"So anyway, can I crash at yours in the spare room or the lounge even, while I look for somewhere else to live?"

Tayla soothes my worries in one go. "Absolutely, as long as you need. Forever. Men are shite. The lot of them." I wonder what happened to make her particularly annoyed this evening.

"Corey and Florian are going as well," I say, studying her reaction.

She pins me with her blue eyes and shakes her pink hair. "Of course, they are. They're all as stupid as each other."

I put my plate and cup down on the coffee table and curl up in a fetal position on the sofa. After these few months with Sam, I'm exhausted. It's been like surfing on waves that are too big for my level of skill. I've fallen one too many times. I drift off to sleep on the sofa with Tayla and Corinne's concerned whispers in the background. The ocean waits for me in disturbed dreams. I'm drowning, and Sam drifts away from me.

I SETTLE BACK into my old routine. Daycare with the kids every day, walking Daisy twice a day, and spending time with Tayla and Corinne in the evenings. They work hard to distract me, and change channels on TV every time there's any mention of the New Zealand team, sailing, or Sam himself.

Nobody asks me anything about Sam at daycare. Even my parents don't mention him. I'm starting to think it was all a dream.

Did we *really* date for several months? Did I meet his parents? Did we move in together? It all seems baffling to me. The only thing that's a constant reminder of him is this dull heartache, that I can't shake off.

Sam's on a crash collision course. He wants to overcome every single thing just to win, to compensate for the loss of Thea. His medal wall, his determination, all make sense. The heartbreak does not.

Corinne keeps assuring me time will heal all wounds, but it's hard not to think about him every day. On my commute to daycare, I allow myself to think about him, about what he could be doing at this time. Is he training? Is he running? Is he thinking about me at all?

* * *

SAM

I try not to think of Ellie when I have breakfast alone every day. I also try not to think about her when I work out at the gym like a maniac for three hours at least each day. I try not to think about her when I shower. I don't think about her when I fall asleep. I most certainly don't drive past the daycare she works at in Takapuna. But then again, I'm a terrible liar.

We trained for a couple of weeks, and I put my head down. After each session, I left, not hanging around with the other guys. They didn't say anything, likely thinking I was rushing to get back to Ellie, which isn't that far from the truth.

We had a one-week break from training, and I thought about visiting my family, but I didn't. If I went by myself, they'd ask uncomfortable questions, and I'm not ready to go there yet. I spent my week studiously avoiding Corey and the other boys, reading, watching every travel documentary Netflix has to offer, and waiting for departure day.

In a cruel twist of fate, I'd chosen to leave on February fourteenth, Valentine's Day of all days. Since Corey and

Florian are both single, they didn't care too much. I suppose now *I'm* single too.

I sigh deeply as I put on the New Zealand team kit and prepare for a media appearance with Corey. I've shaved, but I have huge dark circles under my eyes. It's an outdoor event, so I don't think they'll provide any make-up. I look in the mirror. What you see is what you get today, guys.

I arrive late, so out of character for me.

Corey's annoyed. "Bro, it's just not done, keeping everyone waiting. What were you up to, that you couldn't make it on time?"

"Nothing, bro. Good to see you. Don't see you much these days."

Corey doesn't reply.

We step out in front of the media in our team outfits and are surprised. It's not the usual questions. We're awarded the Corral Cup, an important prize in sailing. Our names will be engraved for eternity onto the side of the silver cup, and the only thing I can think about is whether Ellie is watching on TV. Cameras flash repeatedly, and the film roles never stop.

Corey steps up the mic with a twinkle in his eye and hand placed humbly on his heart. "We're very proud to have achieved this for New Zealand. This is for every child who is thinking about taking up sailing. The ocean's the limit. We thank each and everyone of you for making this possible." Corey, as always, charms the audience.

A reporter reaches a hand up, speaks loudest. "Sam, talk to us. What does this mean to you?"

Oh heck. The journalist caught me off-guard. "It was unexpected, but we're very appreciative."

Cameras flash again. They're giving me a headache.

Another reporter leans forward. "Corey, what are you most excited about: the Sanders Cup, the Olympics, or the Round the World Ocean Race?"

That hits a bit too close to home.

Corey crosses his arms and smiles. "Ah, they're all great challenges, requiring different skills, and we're fortunate to be able to participate in all of them, and expand our skillset. We're proud to be representing New Zealand on all counts."

Like a dog with a bone, they're not letting up. "Sam, tomorrow you're heading off with Corey and Florian Mittel on the Round the World Ocean race for over a year. It's Valentine's Day. How does your girlfriend feel about it?"

I've never been violent in my life, but I could strangle the guy and feed him to seagulls. Corey looks at me intently. I muster some form of self restraint, thinking I need to go to the gym or run a heck of a distance later to burn off some of this anger.

"We're here for this momentous occasion, and it's an amazing achievement not just for us, but for sailing as a sport. Thank you for coming here today to celebrate with us."

Somehow, I manage to bypass the question and wrap the session up neatly with a bow.

I speed out of the building so no journalists catch up to me.

But I can't outrun Corey. He falls into step with me. "Hey, wait up, bro. What was that?"

"What was what?" I feign innocence.

"You know what. You looked like you were going to murder the guy. All good?" I don't like his line of questioning, so I make a hasty escape back to my car.

"All good. See you tomorrow at the airport at 7:00 a.m. sharp." I speed off, leaving Corey full of question marks.

Rats, that was close. What will people think when they watch it back? Did I really look as murderous as I felt? More importantly, will Ellie watch it? Thinking about her makes my chest fill painfully.

Starting tomorrow, I'll be away for a really long time. What I wouldn't give to see her one last time.

Without noticing, my treacherous hands steer towards the Hillcrest highway off-ramp, and I find myself on the way to her house. What the hell am I doing? She doesn't want to see me, she made *that* entirely clear when she left. That dull ache in my chest doesn't let up.

Maybe if I see her again one more time, maybe … I'll be able to think of her less. Like reverse psychology but for a broken heart. Or maybe she'll be etched even more in my memory, and I won't be able to shake this feeling … is it a risk I'm willing to take?

Hillcrest is in stark contrast to Bella Vista. The familiar 1950s houses with their large sections, kids, dogs and mature trees dominate the landscape. No shops, no cafés, no people running, just suburbia.

Before I can make up my mind what I'm doing, I've already turned onto her street. Am I really going to do this?

ELLIE

"Stop barking, Daisy, what's the matter?" Daisy is pretty agitated, and Tayla tries to soothe her. "We're not expecting anyone, are we?" Tayla's looking out the window.

"No, I don't think so. It's too early for Corinne to be back, she said about 10:00 p.m." Corinne had a show at the Opera tonight, and I can't imagine she would have been able to come home early.

Tayla and I are spending the evening at home again, watching Netflix and eating junk food, for my sake.

"Oh, for fuck's sake." Tayla's grumpy but resigned outburst makes me dash to the window.

I gasp. Sam's car is parked up on the other side of the street, and he's just standing there leaning against it. He looks pretty rough under the streetlight—dark circles under his eyes, and a five-o-clock shadow stubbling his face. His Team NZ uniform looks a bit worse for wear.

"Why doesn't this man leave you alone? Isn't he fucking off to Europe tomorrow? Like seriously, he's standing there

169

like a cat in the rain." Tayla's words slice straight through my heart.

I haven't followed any news about the Round the World Ocean Race on purpose. But tomorrow? So soon? And he shows up here after two weeks? Tears fall freely down my cheek, and I hate myself for not being able to look away. I miss him so much. I touch the windowpane, as if I were able to touch him.

Tayla tilts her head and crosses her arms. "What is he doing? He's not even coming up to face you like a man."

Tayla and I watch in horror as he mouths something, maybe Goodbye, then gets into his car and leaves.

CHAPTER 17

SAM

*M*y dad always says better to regret the things you've done, than the things you haven't done. For the last few years, I've tried to live my life in such a way that I regret nothing, particularly after I couldn't rescue Thea. It seems after meeting Ellie last year, I've tossed that philosophy out the window.

I shouldn't have gone to her house yesterday. I shouldn't have stopped across the road. I shouldn't have got out of the car. I shouldn't have stared at Ellie like she was a drink of water in the desert. Then I shouldn't have left without saying a word. She was crying, and I felt like a monster.

She looked more beautiful than ever, even through her tears. I miss her so much, it's like an emptiness that doesn't go away.

This morning I'm in a taxi to the airport, on the way to meet up with Corey and Florian for the Round the World Ocean Race start in Malaga. I've decided I'm going to tell them about the break-up. If there's something affecting my mental state, they deserve to know.

I gather my bags from the taxi, and immediately notice

the hearts, balloons, and banners at the airport, celebrating Valentine's Day. Worst day ever. Can't wait for it to be over. The even worse part is that I'm going to live it twice as we fly through to another time zone.

I check in and move into the special Platinum Elite lounge to wait for the boys, coffee in hand. After not even five minutes, they arrive holding champagne flutes.

"Guys, it's 7:00 a.m. Come on." I can't believe they're starting so early on the booze. I haven't even had breakfast yet.

"Time for celebrating, son. We're going around the world." Corey and Florian clink their glasses, and I sigh.

"Plus, it's Valentine's Day, they were giving them out for free." Florian, ever practical, makes me laugh.

"How's Ellie? Is she coming to Brazil in April?" Corey takes another sip of champagne.

I suppose this is as good a time as any. "Ellie and I ... we broke up a couple of weeks ago." I continue drinking my coffee, trying not to give too much away.

Corey almost drops his champagne flute. "You're kidding. Please tell me you're kidding."

Florian keeps his silence, fixing me with his gaze.

I look at Corey sadly. "It's not going to work, okay. She's working at the preschool. She doesn't want to traipse around the globe, and I ... I don't think it's fair to her. You've always said we're not cut out for relationships. Why are you so put out now? Anyway, I need breakfast."

I get up, go to the buffet, pick at some food, hoping for a respite. Meanwhile Corey and Florian are having an animated discussion. I rejoin them, and the conversation stops. Doesn't bother me.

"So, what are you doing?" Corey's question sounds strange.

"What do you mean what am I doing? I'm eating breakfast, then waiting for the boarding call, then going to Europe with you two losers." I stuff my mouth with another forkful.

Corey clicks his tongue against the roof of his mouth and rolls his eyes. "About Ellie." Am I testing his patience?

"Nothing. She's moved back to Tayla's. I'm on my own. I'll get over it." I sound more optimistic than I feel.

"Sam ..."

The announcer's voice provides a welcome interruption. "Air New Zealand flight 310 to Singapore is now boarding from Gate 2. All passengers please go to gate."

I hastily grab my bag. "That's us." I leg it before Corey or Florian can mention Ellie again.

It's going to be a *long* couple of flights. We're doing Auckland - Singapore, Singapore - London, London - Málaga, with not much time in between. I don't want to go sightseeing. I just want to go to Spain and get on that fucking boat, and put as much distance between me and Ellie as possible.

Corey knows me inside out by now, and when we're sitting together in First Class courtesy of Air New Zealand, Florian right behind us, he can't hold it in any longer. "Sam. I'm worried about you. Like ... really worried about you."

"Nah, all good. I'll be fine. We go to Málaga, start prepping, then head off for a few weeks. Just what the doctor ordered." I'm trying hard to be upbeat.

The more cheerful I try to seem, the more I start believing it's going to be okay, and Ellie will be a distant memory, and I'll get over her like ... like ... Damn. Like *nothing*. I haven't actually had to get over anyone because I've never loved anyone like I loved Ellie.

Like I *love* Ellie.

There it is, that tightness in my chest again. It's not even 9:00 a.m. on the first day away from New Zealand. The time's going to stop, isn't it, every second inching along like a snail race. "I fancy some whisky. When's the lady coming round?"

Corey tosses me a disapproving look. Florian rolls his eyes.

I slump into my seat. "I'll remind you two saints that not even half an hour ago you were guzzling champagne for breakfast. And I've just lost the love of my life, okay, not that you two know what that's like."

Florian scoffs at me. "Oh, is that so? Tell us more. I'm dying to hear it."

I raise an eyebrow just as the flight attendant comes past to take orders. "I'd like a whisky please. Make it a double." I'm belligerent again, and I'll be damned if they're going to make me feel guilty about it.

Corey smiles, showing every single tooth in his head, I swear. "A fruit tea please."

It's my turn to roll my eyes.

"A black tea, no sugar, please." Florian's order is just the icing on the cake.

"Oh, for fuck's sake." I put my headphones on and try to rest, listening to music and ignoring Corey. I can't sleep a wink. Every fucking song makes me think about Ellie. The flight attendant comes back with the whisky glass and some morning tea for us—cheese scones, pastries, dainty sandwiches.

Florian hoovers up the food. "I was starving. Should have had some breakfast back in the lounge." He eyes my plate now.

I pass it to him. At least someone can enjoy it.

Corey's dark gaze fixes on me. "So whose idea was it … the break-up?"

I shake my head in disbelief. "You're not going to let this slide, are you? Why do you even care? Seriously. You weren't even a fan of our relationship. I distinctly recall you badgering me about it making me a worse sailor. Ellie and Tayla being gold diggers. You spout that shit for quite some time." I take a sip of whisky, and it burns my throat. This is a bad idea, and I'll probably pay for it later. But for now, it dulls the ache. I take another sip.

Corey looks into the distance, his thoughts far away. "Let's say I've changed my mind."

"I'm … I don't know what to say, Corey. I genuinely don't know what to say." Corey and I have been sailing together for over fifteen years. Within that time, he's never changed his mind about anything. Whatever persuaded him, it must be powerful.

"Sam …" Florian's voice lifts, subdued, from behind us. "I have a question."

"Not you too, please. Ellie and I have broken up, and that's the end of it." Only sixteen hours left to go, and these two are driving me insane. How many whiskies can I drink in sixteen hours without going into a coma?

"Nah, wasn't going to ask about that. Something else … More personal." Florian's voice is even quieter.

I sigh. "Okay. Ask away. Seems like I won't be able to sleep on this flight with you two nattering away."

"I'm sorry. I just wanted to know … what is it like to make love with someone you're in love with?"

Out of all the questions he could have asked at that particular time I wasn't expecting that one. He could have asked me whether I think there are aliens on Mars, and I wouldn't have found it as strange. Or if Captain Nemo's Nautilus really existed. Or of the Auckland house prices are going up again. Or what shoe size my mother wears.

Corey and I turn to face him at the same time. Corey looks quite comical with a half-eaten pastry lifted halfway to his mouth, and I probably look like a deer caught in headlights.

"Uhhhh … Like … ummm …" I'm lost for words, holding onto my whisky glass for dear life.

"Like how does it feel? Does it feel different than with someone you don't love?" Florian's words make sense, but they also don't make sense. How can it be? Have I had too much whisky on an empty stomach? But I've had breakfast. Maybe I should lie down and try to sleep a bit. It might clear my head.

"Aaaah …" I rub my head and cover my face with my hands. "I really want to know why you're asking me this, but I have a feeling you won't tell me."

Florian nods sadly.

"Uhh … it's different. Very different." I try to find words to describe what Ellie and I shared, and there's nothing that comes to mind to do it justice. But I try. "You want to make the one you love happy and content. You want them to want you just as much as you want them. It's not just about the sex. It's also about companionship … being there in the moment, but also with the future in mind." I must look as miserable as I feel as I turn back around because Corey puts a hand on my shoulder.

"Thank you." Florian's faint voice snaps me out of my own misery. What is he going through that he doesn't want to share? Who is he leaving behind to go away for a whole year?

Corey faces forward in his seat. "You know … when we're back, you could try and beg Ellie to take you back."

I shake my head, take one look out the window, put my earphones back on, and try to sleep again. But I can't. No peace for the brokenhearted, I guess. Is this what it's going to be like for the next year? No sleep and a broken heart won't keep us alive on the ocean. I have to get over this, and fast. Why the hell am I doing this if I'm going to be miserable the whole time? If I'm going to do it—and I am—I have to be committed. It's the adventure of a lifetime! Am I going to let a lost relationship keep me from giving it my all?

Maybe.

No. No. I'm ready for this adventure, whatever it brings. Because if I'm not, my friends could die.

CHAPTER 18

SAM

*I*t's been two weeks since we've arrived in Spain and four weeks since Ellie and I broke up. The emptiness I feel inside hasn't subsided at all, and I still think about her, and what could have been, all the time.

Our Round the World Ocean Race team is called Llorca, after a famous Andalusian poet, and we're all staying at a large hotel in touristy Marbella. Corey, Florian, and I take all available free moments to explore the local area, either by foot, or hiring a car and taking turns to drive.

I soak up the atmosphere in Marbella Old Town, with its quaint squares and tiny bodeguitas offering the most delicious fresh orange juice I've ever had.

The boys and I watch the world go by, and I can't help but think of Ellie from time to time. She would love being here in the sun, trying the food, making conversation with people, buying trinkets. We never got around to going on holiday together.

I wonder what she's doing these days. Is she still at Tayla's? Is she still working at the North Shore daycare? Has she found someone else?

I may or may not have checked her Instagram daily. Corey caught me once, rolled his eyes to high heavens. I also caught him checking Tayla's Instagram, but he denied it. I guess we're even now.

The weather started packing in three days ago and hasn't let up since. There's talk of delaying the start to the race.

This morning, the race director is doing a tour of all the teams' quarters, checking in with everyone. "As you're experienced sailors, you don't need me to come and tell you that these are unsailable conditions."

The breakfast room where we're all gathered is brimming with disapproving sailors whispering their discontent.

The director continues in his clipped British accent. "We're waiting for the go-ahead from the Race Committee, but I'm sorry to say that at this point it doesn't look like we'll be able to start on the first of March as planned. More likely it will be from the seventh of March onwards".

The room is at boiling point by now. I couldn't care less as I'm away from Ellie and everything be damned, but Corey and Florian, among others, are shaking their heads and swearing.

The Director beats a hasty retreat, leaving in a flurry of agitation.

"For fuck's sake, how long are we staying cooped up in here? I'm keen to get going." Corey's impatience is clearly showing. He drums his fingers on the table to a rhythm known only to him.

"I suppose they don't want us to get hurt," I say. "They're being careful. I don't mind waiting," I offer, hoping to lead by example.

Corey lets out a deep sigh. Florian clears his throat and takes a serious drink of coffee.

Jonny, one of the British sailors who is meant to be on our boat, swings by our table.

"Hey lads, all good? Up for a game of Catan to pass away some rainy hours?" He's cheerful and carefree, and for once I wish I were in his shoes. No visible past traumas, maybe no girlfriends left behind.

Florian perks up. "We need a couple more for Catan. Do you think you can rally some other guys?"

Jonny laughs. "Sure do. There's three of us Brits plus two Kiwis and a German here. Reckon we have enough."

I'd hoped to go exploring some more in the area since we couldn't train or depart, but the constant rain has smothered that idea. Maybe a morning of board games might make the time go faster, and I'm keen to meet others who love sailing as much as I do.

Corey stays silent but follows us to a bigger table, so I gather he's participating. We join Jonny, Cam, and Phil—the British contingent—at the table.

Jonny takes charge. "Right folks, do you know the rules?"

We all nod.

I'm a bit rusty, I haven't played board games since ... since I took Ellie to my parents' house at Christmas. I scratch my head. My chest tightens. Ooof. I haven't told them yet. They're going to be disappointed. If I tell them today, that gives them a year and then some to get over the breakup, to forgive me. Not likely. Not sure even I'll have forgiven myself by then.

"...Ten points to win the game. The winner gets a bottle of whisky of their choice." Everyone laughs at that, but it seems I must have missed a joke.

Corey's relaxed now, cracking jokes with the others and being his usual charming self. Even Florian chimes in from time to time to make fun of my game choices.

"So, what brings you here, guys? For a year-long race?" Phil, the older British sailor, asks, a loaded question if I've ever heard one.

"I want to win." The words are out of my mouth, before I realize what I'm saying. I've always wanted to win. Winning means I'm alive. Winning means I'm worthy ... I look down before I say something stupid.

Phil laughs. "Of course you do. We all do."

Corey's looking straight at me. "Not as much as he does."

I'm two thirds of the way to my victory points, and the others are starting to cotton on that I'm on track to win the game.

"Hey, that's not fair. Block him." Cam, a British sailor in their early 20s, tries in vain to rally the troops.

Corey rolls his eyes. "Nah, that's what he's like, wants to win every time." Corey just sounds resigned. "If only he were so determined in his *personal life*." He raises an eyebrow at me.

"Whoaaaa." Johny wiggles his eyebrows. "Loving this. What's he hiding?" Jonny is having a whale of a time, and everyone at the table is staring at me.

I hate it. "That was below the belt, Corey." The last thing I want is to talk about Ellie. The thought of her torments me enough every night and every waking moment, thank you very much. I don't need Corey's help to feel shite.

I gain two more victory points plus a bonus and win the game in just under two hours. Everyone else is deflated.

Corey's got more up his sleeve. "To answer your earlier question, Phil, I think we're all here to run away or hide from something." I don't even have to look up to know his gaze is fixed on me. "Maybe a broken heart ... maybe money ... maybe just restlessness ... maybe just the desire to win ... But at the end of the day, if your heart's not in it, then you shouldn't do it."

I can't look him in the eye. I just can't. It's all too raw.

But Corey won't let me run. "Look at me, Sam. Just look

at me. I'll tell you two things, just two, then you can tell me to go to hell."

I look at him. He's the same old Corey, my sailing partner since we were sixteen and eighteen, respectively. In my mind's eye, he hasn't aged that much since we were teens, though we're now in our 30s. Maybe more wrinkles, more gray hairs, and a heck of a lot more experience.

Everyone else is silent, probably wondering what this is all about. Florian is drinking a third coffee already.

Corey puts up a single finger, holds it high. "First thing. You win this race. And then? What's the point of winning this race? And the next one? And the one after that? What's the point of winning any of them, if you've lost the most important thing, the love of your life?"

I feel like leaving. It's just too much. I can't bear it. My knuckles are white and my fingernails slice into my palms.

Corey adds a second finget to his first. "And second, and last thing, this thing you've been looking for may be at home in New Zealand ..."

Phil wipes a tear from the corner of his eye. Cam clears their throat, and Jonny's smile has disappeared.

Corey's on a roll. "Now you can tell me to go to hell, but I've been wanting to tell you this for the past two weeks because you're miserable. I've known you for fifteen years, and I've never seen you this unhappy." Corey's talking so fast now, I can't keep up.

My voice is too quiet. "I don't know what to do. I've never done it before."

Florian's voice rings out clearly. "You need to go back to New Zealand and abandon the race."

He says it like it's the easiest thing in the world. Abandon the race. Go home. And my heart seems to agree. At the end of it all, I'd rather win Ellie than a race. "Alright."

ELLIE

It's been two weeks since Sam came to our house, and stood outside without coming in, before leaving for Europe the next day. I still have nightmares about it from time to time, his face full of sorrow as he drove away.

I'm still at Tayla's house, in the spare room, after Corinne took my old room. I haven't found a place that's as nice as this one, and I enjoy the company of friends.

Tayla and Corinne keep me sane and grounded. Whenever I start crying, reminiscing about Sam and I, they distract me without trying to push me to date someone else.

Today's an ordinary Thursday, and after coming in from work, I change into leggings and a t-shirt, and take Daisy out for a walk. Daisy motors on with her chunky legs every time I throw the ball and dutifully brings it back. After a solid hour of time together, I go back, and prepare to make dinner for all of us, as it's my turn to cook.

Before they come home, I turn the TV on, a little bit of background noise to keep me company while I'm cooking. I prepare to roast the fish, and my heart skips a beat. There are images of Sam and Corey on TV. My first instinct is to turn it off. Seeing him brings me so much fresh pain, but it seems I'm a sucker for pain so I turn the volume up.

"Sam Northcroft, the famed Kiwi Sailing champion and Olympian, is pulling out of the Round the World Ocean Race for personal reasons. Fellow sailors Corey Fine and Florian Mittel are still in the competition. Northcroft's replacement will be announced soon."

I droop onto the sofa just as Tayla and Corinne enter the house. They see my stricken expression and immediately rally around me.

Tayla leans and touches my shoulder. "What's wrong? Has something happened?"

A twist in my gut. Fear. Relief. Apprehension. Doubt. Love. "I don't know." I burst into tears. "He's coming back."

CHAPTER 19

SAM

I'd forgotten it only takes fifteen minutes to drive from my house to Ellie's. In my mind the Harbor Bridge that separates our places is an uncrossable gulf, impossible to overcome. Fifteen minutes, three songs on the radio, or a short sailing regatta.

I am buzzing with excitement at seeing Ellie again, holding her in my arms, telling her how I felt, and this feeling buoyed me until Shanghai. There's no place like home, and I've come to learn that home is wherever Ellie is.

But doubts drown my high. Maybe she found someone else already. Maybe she won't want to see me at all. Maybe I'm entitled, thinking I can slot straight back into her life and pick up where we left off.

I haven 't thought about what to tell her when I see her. In the best scenario, she just falls into my arms, tells me she loves me and that she's been waiting for me. In the worst scenario, she slams the door in my face.

It's evening, and the setting sun mottles colors in the harbor. Before I have a chance to process everything, I'm in Hillcrest, with its quiet tree-lined streets. Could I live here?

There's nothing keeping me City side. It's not like I go out every night. Or every week. Or every month, even.

I park on Ellie and Tayla's driveway. The lights are off in the front part of the house. Have they gone out? I haven't prepared for this. What should I do next? Should I write an old-fashioned note and push it through the letterbox? Should I text her and tell her I want to see her? I turn to leave and catch a glimmer of light at the back of the house. My heart leaps. They must be in the garden.

I lock my car and walk towards the garden side gate. There's laughter, some music ... and is that a man's voice? What the hell is going on? I'm torn between turning back to my car and running away like I always do. But a new feeling creeps through my chest—jealousy. Why are there guys here, and what are they doing? I walk faster and open the gate to a scene I hadn't expected when I left Spain and abandoned the race.

It's like I'm in a sit-com, and I'm the new arrival in town everyone stares at. I take a good look at everyone around the table. Some are familiar faces like Ellie, Tayla, Paddy and Gracie. Other faces are unfamiliar. I suspect the dark-haired girl is Corinne, but the guy next to Ellie gives me pause. Have I met him before? Is he one of their friends? I can't place my finger on it, but maybe we've met. They're all silent, staring at me with their mouths open, about to eat dinner, and I've just interrupted them. Great.

Ellie looks even more mouthwateringly beautiful than I remembered. My heart skips a beat.

Paddy recovers quickly and lets out a hearty laugh. "Well, I'll be damned, if it isn't the prodigal son. Hey cuz, good to see you back in one piece. Looking good. A bit on the light side, though."

This is probably the worst-case scenario, one I hadn't prepared for, where Ellie not only isn't alone, but is surrounded by a bunch of clowns. And that chief clown, the dude by her side.

Tayla rolls the wine in her glass lazily. "Watcha doing?" Her voice is calm, but she's lethal, that's clear. "All swell?"

I look straight at Ellie. "Hey. Ah, I was hoping to speak to Ellie, maybe take her out for dinner … But you guys are already eating. Maybe I should come back another time."

Ellie is agitated. I can't read other people's expressions, but I feel so in tune with her now, that I can tell broadly how she's feeling.

Corinne gestures toward an empty chair. "Just get a chair and have a sausage sandwich. Lord knows you look like you need it." More humor. Great. I'm being roasted mercilessly, but I guess I deserve it.

The guy next to Ellie laughs politely, as well, and my fist bunches. Gracie nudges Paddy, who notices the change in atmosphere and takes pity on me.

"Ellie, how about you take Daisy out for *another* walk, and Sam here can make sure you're safe?" I fervently give thanks to Paddy in my head. I'll buy him the most expensive whisky I can get my hands on. I don't know exactly what I'll tell Ellie, but I know that I need a chance.

"Talk it out," Gracie whispers, but loud enough for everyone to hear.

Ellie's been silent so far. She looks at Tayla, who shakes her head in annoyance. She stands up, and her floor length summer dress flows around her. Without saying a word, she grabs Daisy's lead and sets off towards the gate, Daisy hot on her heels. I follow suit, like a drowning man chasing a mermaid. Just being near her after being apart for nearly a month is everything. And not enough. I need to know. Will she give me another chance, or will she send me to hell?

ELLIE

*S*am looks different, somehow. His hair is shorter, and his body is leaner. He doesn't seem nervous at all. He stood his ground as nearly everyone at the table had a go at him.

In my wildest dreams I hadn't imagined him casually dropping by. Of course I've wondered what personal reasons brought him home. Maybe something happened to his family to make him leave the Round the World Ocean Race.

As we walk side by side with Daisy towards the park around the corner from my house, I steal glances at him. He's smartly dressed, and he's got a determination about him that I haven't seen before.

"Is your family well?" We enter the park and I let Daisy off the lead so she can have a sniff around the place.

Sam's surprised. He clearly wasn't expecting this question. "Yes, all well back home. Why do you ask?"

We get to a bench that's a bit out of the way, by the shrubbery towards the pond, and Sam gestures for me to sit.

I sit and search his face. "Why did you come back early

from the Round the World Race then?" I brace myself for the answer, however painful it may be.

His gray eyes are stormy by now, and I can read many things in them. Need. Hope. Abandon. I let myself hope for the first time since I heard he quit the race.

"I think you know ... I came back for you." He picks up my hand, brings it to his lips, kissing my fingers one by one, and sending shivers down my spine.

"Why?" I just can't make sense of this. One moment he goes away, next moment he comes back, like passing ships through the night. I take my hand away.

He pushes his fingers through his hair and frowns. "You're not going to make this easy, are you?" He grins.

I just raise my eyebrows at him.

He shifts a bit and rubs his palms on his pants. "I don't know how to make grand gestures. I can't make fancy speeches and charm everybody. What I do know is I've been the most miserable I've ever been in my life over the past month, and I need you in my life. You're my North Star. I'm lost at sea without you."

Oh my ... Whatever resolve I have is fading away bit by bit, thawing like an ice cube left in the sun. Yet ... "You were hell-bent on going on that year-long journey around the world. What do you really want?" I'm scared it's going to happen again, and I'll go through all the pain over and over again with each new race, like *Groundhog Day*. It was enough last time, and I'm still not over it.

He smiles. "At home and on the way here I rehearsed everything I would say ... I was going to take you out for dinner somewhere private, and I was going to tell you how I've felt all this time, how much I love you, and that I know what I want to do ... But now I'm here with you, I'm lost for words." Sam takes my hand again, moves closer to me on the bench, and looks deep into my eyes. "I've behaved like an absolute dick. Your job is much more important than mine. You teach kids about numbers, sharks, and … stuff." Sam looks away and waves a hand towards the east side, where the sea is. "I just make boats go fast and get paid for it. Not on the same level, Ellie. Not by far."

I reach for him and open my mouth to speak.

His gaze pins me again, before I get a chance to say anything. "I've always wanted to do that race, probably since I first heard of it …"

His words leave me breathless, like the air I'm inhaling is made out of shards of glass.

"But it was just another thing to win, to conquer. Winning, that race or any other, won't bring Thea back." Sam rubs the back of his head with a thoughtful look. "Not only will it not bring her back, but I'll lose much more. I'll still have to be away from time to time, like for the Olympics … But I want *this* life. You, me, Daisy. Walks in the park. A home. I want a chance to make things right."

In the twilight, the end of a summer breeze gently caresses the trees. It feels like a moment trapped in time— Daisy chasing Monarch butterflies, the sound of the leaves, the scent of Wisteria, and Sam's full attention on me. There's a lot at stake.

"What do *you* want, Ellie?"

His soft voice hits a note within me. My heart swells, and I'm ready to cry. I want Sam. I cup his face and lean in for a kiss. Hot tears streak my face as he moves closer still, wraps his arms around me, and sends my senses spinning. I haven't felt him this close for over four weeks now, and the nearness of him overwhelms me. He smells and tastes like the ocean, and I'm powerless to resist.

We kiss for what feels like forever, rediscovering each

other, hands exploring with a lazy urgency. He pulls me onto his lap, and my long dress catches on a loose screw on the bench. Sam sighs in frustration and helps me untangle it, but his hands are shaking so he's making a hash job of it. I try and fail to contain my laughter of relief.

His gaze is hooded with want. "I missed you." As he frees my dress, he slips a hand underneath and cups my ass. I gasp at his touch on my bare skin.

"Shh …" He silences me with a kiss. His hand moves to my hip then trails lazily upwards, settling on my thigh. All my senses are on edge, but I want more. I wiggle on his lap, feeling his hardness through the layers of fabric. We're both wearing too many clothes.

I'm so tightly strung by his touch, I'm practically panting now. "Someone may see us."

Sam kisses my neck and his hand reaches further between my thighs. "I don't think so." His fingers move gently, first over my panties, then full on stroking my clit in a rhythm that makes me slowly lose my mind. I'm about to come hard, so I grasp his shirt and kiss him to stop myself from screaming out loud as I ride the waves of sensation.

I'm sure I have a satisfied smile on my face, and I couldn't care less. "Now it's your turn."

Sam kisses my nose, my cheeks and forehead, then holds me close. "I'm *very* uncomfortable, but the others will be wondering where we are. We should head back." Regret drenches every one of his words.

"How about … you sit down for dinner with everyone— sausage, bread and tomato ketchup …"

Sam laughs. "The food of champions."

"And then … you stay the night."

His gray eyes darken again. "Are you sure it's a good idea? Small house. Tayla and Corinne there as well." He shrugs his shoulders.

"As long as we're quiet." I kiss his jaw.

He laughs wholeheartedly. "I'm quiet. Are you?"

I get up off his lap, straighten my dress and my hair, pick up the lead, and call for Daisy. "My lips are sealed." A walk back home from the park. Just another ordinary day. But it feels like the beginning of our story.

***

SAM

I'm aching for Ellie. I've never wanted anything or anyone as much as I want her at this moment. You could dangle the Sanders Cup in front of me, and I'd let it fall to the ground if it meant I get to be with Ellie.

What happened in the park was definitely unplanned. I'm thirty-two but around her I'm like a hormonal teenager. As we walk towards her house, it dawns on me that the others will have a field day with this.

While we've straightened up our clothes, I'm missing a button off my now VERY rumpled shirt, and Ellie looks deliciously tousled, like she was thoroughly kissed or maybe more. At least we haven't tumbled around and got grass stains.

This is one I'm going to have to take on the chin. But it may give that other dude some pause. We get back before I get a chance to ask Ellie who he is and how he came to be at the dinner.

We go through the gate, and when they see the state of us, Paddy and Gracie burst out laughing. Tayla, Corinne, and the other guy raise their eyebrows.

I quickly sit at the table. "I'm starving. Do you guys have any food left?"

Paddy wheezes from so much glee. "He's starving! Love it."

Ellie looks puzzled. I guess she hasn't noticed my shirt or hadn't thought it was a big deal. She sits next to me, and I immediately place a hand on her leg.

Gracie adds fuel to the fire. "We've never seen him like this. It's cute. We're enjoying it."

The new guy stands up to make a hasty retreat. "Guys, I have to be up early tomorrow morning to open up the clinic. It was fun, let's do it again sometime soon."

"Don't go, Alex! We haven't even introduced you to Sam, though I think you've probably met before." Ellie's words make me do a double take. How could I have met him, where? Clinic? What clinic?

"Sam, this is Alex, Sophie's brother. He's a veterinarian up here on The Shore." The penny drops loud and clear. I stand up and shake his hand.

"Sorry man, I didn't recognize you. You were at my brother's wedding three years ago. Let's catch up over a drink sometime."

He shakes my hand, nods, and waves. Well, there's nothing to say he wasn't interested in Ellie. I reserve judgement.

Gracie winks at us. "We're heading off as well, leaving you lovebirds behind. Come to dinner sometime soon."

Gracie hugs each and every one of us, and I whisper in her ear. "Thanks Gracie, appreciate it. I mean it."

Paddy winks at me and flicks my missing shirt button-hole. "Until next time, champ." He's not going to let me live this one down.

They leave, and I find myself stared down by Tayla and Corinne.

Tayla doesn't mince words. "'Spose you're going to stay the night."

"Yes, I am, if Ellie will have me."

Ellie covers my hand with her hand and smiles.

Corinne pokes my chest. "Pull a nasty trick like that again, and we'll cut your ball sack and serve it back to you on a silver plate. Understood?"

I laugh, but I'm definitely a little bit nervous. "Understood."

Tayla turns back before leaving the room. "How was Corey?" She tries to be nonchalant about it.

Ellie and Corinne look at her with their eyebrows raised.

I've got interesting information for her. "He was well. Will be back next year. Last time I saw him he was checking out your Instagram." Not exactly true, but I did catch him once checking her profile out. Maybe he did it more often than I thought.

Tayla laughs. "That ratbag. Ok folks, I'm going to bed. Sam and Ellie can do the washing up since they fucked off for most of the dinner." Corinne joins her and they head into the house.

Ellie and I are left behind in the garden with twinkling lights. Daisy is asleep, tired after her long evening walk.

Ellie's looking down, long eyelashes casting shadows on her face in the fading sunlight. "Are you going to regret staying behind?" Her voice comes from far away, though she's sitting right next to me.

"Regret? No way. For once, staying out of a race is the best thing that's ever happened to me."

Ellie turns towards me, a smile blossoming on her face, and I feel like I won the biggest prize of all.

CHAPTER 20

SAM

From March until September when Corey comes back, I just want to take it easy. For me taking it easy means juggling less balls, but still juggling.

I try out a new sailing boat class for competing, see how I get on by myself. I speak at various sailing and marine conservation events. I go to physio for old injuries. I visit my parents and Ellie's parents.

More importantly, there isn't a single day or night Ellie and I aren't together. I'm relishing this time. It will soon be interrupted. The Sanders Cup events are coming up this December, and the Olympics are next year, which means we won't be able to spend as much time together. Though the schedule isn't as grueling as the Round the World Race, and Ellie promised to join me for the Olympics.

In April I sold my Bella Vista home; it just didn't feel right anymore. Ellie and I looked together for somewhere to buy on the North Shore until we found a gem with direct beach access. In the mornings, I take my kayak and paddle around the gulf, for calm and perspective. When I'm at the mercy of the ocean, it's easier to think. To breathe.

From our new home, Ellie's able to walk to work. She's progressed to become Team Lead, and I'm very proud of her. Bonus, we're about fifteen minutes away from Tayla and Corinne or Paddy and Gracie. I enjoy the quieter pace, and Ellie shines with happiness.

After Ellie left for work this morning, I made a couple of important calls, and now I'm on my way for my 10:30 a.m. appointment, one I wouldn't miss for the world.

ELLIE

I'm at Corinne and Tayla's, sipping a chai latte. "I'm not a psychic, but sometimes I just *know*, okay. Sam's got something to hide."

Corinne and Tayla share knowing smiles.

"Out with it, you two. What's going on?"

Tayla shrugs, but her smile doesn't change. "Don't know. Haven't seen anything. Haven't heard anything. As far as I'm concerned, it's nothing."

Corinne examines her purple and gold nails.

I don't think I'll be able to extract anything out of these two, though it's clear they know something. I get an idea. "Have you heard from Corey?" Now I've got Tayla's attention.

She glances at me then looks away.

"Of course you have. What's he up to? All well up there on the high seas?"

Tayla blows hair out of her rolling eyes. "None of your fucking business, babe."

I stand. I've got to get going, but I'm not letting this bone go yet. I smile as I slip toward the garden gate. "Not long now. A few months?"

Tayla sighs, and I don't pursue this. It's obvious something's going on in that tennis court.

Corinne laughs.

I waggle my eyebrows. "I'm off. Speak to you soon. Let's do something girly together. Instagram friendly."

Tayla waves me off.

* * *

WHEN I GET BACK to our new place, it dawns on me what's changed. Sam is more secretive. With his phone, his things, his appointments. Neither of us are the jealous type, and it's never occurred to me to check his phone, nor has he given me any reasons. Until now that is.

I turn the key in the lock. "I'm baaack." Daisy greets me, aquiver with excitement. To her, it doesn't matter whether I've been gone an hour, five hours, or five days. She's always happy to see me. I give her a few pats then go through to the main living area.

"I'm in here." Sam's voice echoes through the hallways.

Something smells delicious. There's Sam, cooking something following a recipe on YouTube. His cooking has definitely improved in the time we've been living together again.

I embrace him from behind. "What'cha cookin'?"

He turns around and lifts me up for a kiss. "Crayfish risotto."

"Judging by the smell, it's going to be divine. How was your day?" I look at him closely to see if I can glean any behavior change.

He lets me go and turns away. "It was good. Lots of things ticked off the list. What about yours?"

Has he always been this evasive? It must be a new thing. Maybe I'm right that something's changed. Another woman perhaps? I give myself a mental shake and try firmly not to go down that route.

I change tack. "Have you heard from Corey at all in the past few weeks?"

He turns in surprise. "Strange you should mention it, but I spoke with him this morning. He's docking in Hong Kong, nearly halfway on the race."

"Is he well? Turns out Tayla heard from him as well. She didn't want to say anything, and I was just being nosy as usual."

Sam laughs and stirs some more white wine into the risotto. "He's well. Something happened though. On one of the boats. The race has been cut short, and he's due back the second of September. Interesting about Tayla, though."

I shrug my shoulders then turn on the TV to check out the news, still pondering Sam's change in attitude.

* * *

I SLEPT VERY BADLY last night, tossed and turned, and disturbed Sam a lot. He held me close for part of the night, but I pushed him away. Either too hot or too cold, or just simply worrying about what's brought these feelings on. By sunrise, I'm resolute that I need to confront him, to put this idea to rest, or at least give him a chance to come clean if something's truly up.

I put a hoodie over my short pajamas, put some flip flops on, and prepare to take Daisy for an early walk on the beach.

I thought Sam was still asleep, but he springs out of bed, and puts on a t-shirt, shorts and hoodie. He's headed my direction, but I'm out the gate and on the beach, Daisy sprinting off, before he can reach me.

Sam trots after me. "Wait up! I'm coming with you." He's unshaven and looks a bit rough around the edges. His auburn hair is aglow as the sun rises above the sea.

"Only you could look this good at sunrise, Sam. I haven't had coffee and I feel zombified." We laugh. "What's your secret?"

He stops dead in his tracks, and I stop as well. Oh no. Is this where he tells me …

"Ah, Ellie, I … want to ask you something." Sam kneels on the beach and takes a ring out of his pocket. I think I'm going to faint.

"Uh … will you marry me?"

I cover my mouth so I don't scream.

He rubs the back of his head, his face a mix of concern and anxiety. "If it's too soon … I can wait."

"No, no, no, don't wait. Absolutely not. YES. Of course, as if there would be any other answer in this whole world."

He stands, and I throw myself at him. We kiss under the blazing sunrise with Daisy circling us in a happy dance.

I try the ring on, and it fits perfectly. It's a gorgeous antique, just like the bracelet he got me for Christmas. He seems to have his sources, and they're very good. I file away a mental note to find out who this mysterious jeweler is.

We walk back towards the house, and I can't wait to let my parents know, and the girls, but a thought is nagging me. "Is this why you were being so secretive lately? I thought you'd found someone else."

His laughter silences my doubts. "As if I'd ever want anyone else."

EPILOGUE

SAM

"*I* must say, if anyone had told me this time last year that I'd be Best Man at your wedding, I would have told them to lay off the booze."

Everybody laughs at Corey's remarks, particularly my side of friends and family. He's dressed to the nines in navy suit trousers, white shirt, and beige waistcoat, with his sleeves rolled up.

"Ellie, now put your hand on the table please." Corey gestures to us. "Now, Sam, put your hand over hers." Ellie has small, delicate hands. Mine are big, full of calluses and generally unappealing. Where's Corey going with this?

"Enjoy this moment," he says, "because this will be the last time you have the upper hand, my friend."

Guffaws ensue, and even Ellie finds this funny.

Good ol' Corey, eh, working the room. It was obvious from the beginning I'd ask him to be my Best Man, even after what happened two weeks ago, right after he came back from the Round the World Ocean Race early.

Corey motions for the crowd to settle down, and they do. "I'm ending my speech on a serious note to say I'm very happy you've found your soulmate in Ellie. She's a rare one, and you've got to treasure her. Parteeeey on now, people." He rounds the table towards us and gives me a hug.

"I'm going to miss you, man." Corey's being surprisingly emotional.

"I'm not leaving anywhere. Glad you're back, bro. We're still doing the Sanders Cup in three months' time and the Olympics in nine months." We have a tight schedule, which means I won't be able to take Ellie on honeymoon until after the Olympics.

"You know what I mean. You've said goodbye to the single life."

Is he drunk? Again? He doesn't stumble but his eyes look feverish. I can feel myself getting angry. On my *wedding day*. "No more drinking today, okay. I don't want a repeat of what happened two weeks ago." His eyes look hurt for a moment, but he shakes it off.

"Nah, bro, all good." Corey pats me on the back, signs peace out, and goes to mingle with guests. He stops to say hi to his two brothers.

I scan the outdoor area for Ellie. She should be easy to spot. She's the only one in a white dress, but with these lights flashing, and constant noise, it's hard to keep my brain in check. I take a deep breath and tap my wrist, like Ellie taught me, and I spot her by the bar. She's my lighthouse in a storm, so I make my way towards her. As always.

* * *

ELLIE

*C*orinne wears the most fashionable hat I've ever seen, all feathers and geometrical shapes, putting the mother of the bride, my mum, to shame. She's sipping on our signature wedding cocktail, and checking out the eligible bachelors. "I don't know *how* you pulled off all of this in such a short time. It's totes amazing."

She's right. As soon as Sam proposed, we both knew it would have to be at my parents' winery in Matakana. Private, intimate, family-oriented, and very much *us*. My aunts traveled from the UK, his nana is here with her carer, even Corey brought part of his family along.

I sip my wine. "At least the venue was sorted, and the stars aligned, so the fifteenth of September it was." I'm feeling self-conscious in my wedding dress. It's definitely the most expensive outfit I've ever worn in my life, but Sam's face alone was worth the price as he watched my father walked me down the aisle.

I scan the small crowd. "Where's Tayla? I haven't seen her in a while." But I see my husband coming towards us. "Hey husband. Have you seen Tayla?"

He kisses me gently to not smudge my makeup. What a gem. Corinne waves and moves away to get some more drinks.

"No, wife. She must be around. I'm looking for Corey. I hope he hasn't had too much to drink." Sam looks concerned, and he's got every right to be, after what happened two weeks ago. It could jeopardize everything, from their entry at the Olympics, to their income. I try not to think about it.

Then, out of the blue, Tayla emerges from the vines, followed by Corey, both looking a picture. Tayla's makeup is smudged, and Corey's light-colored waistcoat has green marks on it.

I burst out laughing. "No fucking way. Look." I nod towards them.

Sam's just as shocked as I am. "What the heck. What's going on? What were they up to?"

I whisper in Sam's ear. "You know exactly what they were up to."

He puts his arms around me and scatters kisses from my jawline, to my lips, to my neck.

I gasp softly.

He chuckles. "Let's take this party somewhere else, Mrs. Northcroft." Sam picks me up and carries me as if I weigh no more than a feather.

"Don't mind if we do, Mr. Northcroft." I'll never get enough of Sam.

We're looking at a future of love, and it feels like sailing into an unknown ocean together, a little scary and a lot exciting. The adventure of a lifetime.

* * *

THE SERIES CONTINUES with *Hidden Deep* (*New Zealand Sailing Book 2*).

Sign up to Trinity Wood's newsletter for a copy of *Making Waves*, a novelette featuring some of your favorite characters in this series.

If you enjoyed *Learning to Love*, please consider leaving a review.

ACKNOWLEDGEMENT

A huge thanks to my husband for the grounding and support. You're the funniest person I know. No, you are. No, YOU ARE. Also a thought for my kiddos, without whom this book would have been written and published much faster. Lots of love to my extended family.

Lots of love to my Romance Cafe family who have been by my side every damn step of the way, and who are excited I'm *finally* publishing something of my own. Thank you Anna, Shanti, Katherine, Sofia, Rachel, Jenny, and Lisa. Thank you for everything, Liana.

Thank you to Becky for providing insights on waterfalls in Auckland, to Calina and Iulia for discussing knots over cocktails, to Caro and Petrus for cheering me on even on bad days. Thank you to Lauriel for many things, among them being a reminder that the sun rises from the East and sets to the West.

Thank you to Whitney for endless patience. You're the best!

This book wouldn't have happened at all without the

huge support I've received over the past few years from the Romance community. You all rock, keep empowering, lifting, and fixing each other's crowns.

ABOUT THE AUTHOR

Trinity writes contemporary romance set in New Zealand. Because she can't get enough of book boyfriends, she created some of her own. Get ready to meet Sam, Corey, Jay, Tai, Luke, Mike, Travis, and many more, but please form an orderly line. Behind Trinity.

A self-professed good-time nerd, Trinity's never far away from one of her trusty Pokemon coffee mugs. Trinity also swears that Margaritas can cure colds.

9 780473 581435